PRAISE FOR **THE 8TH CONTINENT** SERIES:

"**Fast-paced action**, cool inventions and remarkable robots."
—*Kirkus Reviews*

"**Good fun** in the tradition of M. T. Anderson's Pals in Peril series."
—*Booklist*

"**Zippy pace** and **original premise**."
—*School Library Journal*

"London's **smart and humorous** series launch hurtles along at a . . . knuckle-whitening pace. Kids will especially enjoy George's outlandish robotic and vehicular inventions—including 2-Tor, the siblings' giant mechanical crow teacher—in this fun yet thought-provoking story."
—*Publishers Weekly*

"This is a delightful start to the adventures of the Lane family, with their flying tree and their mechanical bird tutor. Evie and Rick and their brilliant if eccentric parents are **wonderfully vivid**, and the villains who try to impede them in their quest to save the Earth, equally **memorable.** It's all in the great tradition of adventure fiction for young readers, running back through Akiko and Freddy the Pig all the way to Tom Sawyer."
—Kim Stanley Robinson, author of *Red Mars*

WE BUILT THIS CITY

THE 8TH CONTINENT

MATT LONDON

razOr
bill

An Imprint of Penguin Random House

THE

WE BUILT THIS CITY

8

TH

BUILD IT.

RUN IT.

RULE IT.

MATT LONDON

CONTINENT

razOr
bill

An Imprint of Penguin Random House
Penguin.com

ISBN: 978-1-59514-840-7

Printed in the United States of America

1 3 5 7 9 10 8 6 4 2

For my family

DARKNESS SURROUNDED VESUVIA PIFFLE LIKE A SEWER TANK OF ICE WATER.

It was not the first time she had been cruelly and wrongfully imprisoned, but after her mother betrayed and abandoned her, what else should she have expected? She was completely and utterly alone.

The door opened. That scrape of metal on metal, an agonized scream, stung her ears. Rusted hinges whined. A blade of light widened across her face, piercing her eyes. When she covered her eyes in pain, the spots remained, white and sparkling.

"Get off the floor, you little rat. Time Out is over." That voice. Colder than the metal floor, darker than the room around her, that voice she knew so well. Mister Dark.

She cowered in the corner, hiding from him.

"I trust you've learned your lesson. Now it's time to come upstairs and be a good little employee for Mastercorp."

With a growl like a caged animal, she rose from her corner and stomped toward him, her anger fueling a sudden burst of strength. "I'm no one's employee! I am the CEO of Condo Corp!"

Mister Dark grimaced like a wolf who didn't like the taste of his latest meal. He took a step back, away from the pale blond-haired girl. "The Condo Corporation has been absorbed by Mastercorp. Hostile takeover. You are the Chief Executive Officer of a company that no longer exists."

"No!" she shrieked, spinning angrily and stomping on the hard floor. "You must be stupider than you look if you think I'm going to let a department store mannequin like you take away my company. I won't let you!"

"Condo Corp is gone, and outbursts like this are why you got locked up down here in the first place, Vesuvia." Mister Dark tugged at his collar, revealing bulging silver veins on his muscular neck. The silver veins pulsed with a strange power. Mister Dark winced in pain as his hand accidentally brushed against a vein.

"What's wrong with you? That looks disgusting." Vesuvia felt like she was going to yack.

Mister Dark produced a clear plastic vial filled with silver liquid from his coat pocket. "I have been ingesting regular doses of a serum of my own design. The primary ingredient is Anti-Eden Compound."

"So you're using that chemical cocktail that turns organic matter into trash to transform your insides into metal. Seems smart." And by smart she meant super dumb. Vesuvia stuck out her tongue.

"It is very smart. Coated in metal, my bones are

unbreakable, my muscles indefatigable. By drinking a small dose every day, I am immunizing myself to the raw Anti-Eden Compound. Watch." He tilted back his head and swallowed the contents of the vial. The silver streaks of his neck veins grew swollen. His muscular arms and legs bulged. Mister Dark made a fist, then, without even a glance, punched the wall beside him. The clang was so loud Vesuvia clutched her head. The single punch created a foot-wide crater in the wall. Mister Dark removed his hand from the dent and examined the meteor attached to his wrist. "You see?"

"Looks painful," Vesuvia muttered.

Mister Dark smiled in a way that fit his name. "Come. Your mother is waiting."

The Mastercorp dreadnought was eight hundred meters in length, a portable headquarters for the military-industrial corporation. Shaped like a massive black shark, the flying submarine was stuffed teeth to tail with weapons, soldiers, and scientific testing facilities. In her time as a Mastercorp employee, working for her mother, Mastercorp's Vice President of Research & Development and the Director of Eighth Continent Activities, Vesuvia often explored the twisting halls of the vessel, seeking a quiet place to be alone. But if she was really being honest with herself, what she had been looking for was an escape hatch. That was one thing she never found.

On their way through the ship, Vesuvia and Mister Dark passed pairs of worker-bots doing maintenance on the dreadnought's propulsion and energy systems. Vesuvia had forgotten how much she had missed fiddling with her hot-pink robo-bird guardian, Didi, and other Mastercorp machines. Squads of Mastercorp soldiers strutted down the halls in their angular uniforms. Even if they weren't pink, the black uniforms looked snappy. Thanks to her extended Time Out in the dreadnought holding cell, Vesuvia couldn't remember the last time she had gone shopping. Ugh, life was so unfair!

Mister Dark guided her to the docking bay, where boats, submarines, and hoverships were stored between excursions. Mrs. Piffle stood at a black metal podium addressing a trio of children who looked about Vesuvia's age, but something about them was not exactly human. Bulky metal protrusions grew off them at weird angles, giving them a vague resemblance to different animals. There was a girl whose prosthetic legs looked like the hind limbs of a cheetah, a buzzard with wings that enveloped his slender, sickly body, and a small boy in glasses who was protected by a cybernetic shell like a hermit crab. It was like a gang of fifth graders had teamed up to dress as Vesuvia's beloved Piffle Pink Patrol, her squadron of robotic animals, for Halloween.

If Vesuvia's mother noticed her daughter, she did not show it. She spoke to the other children in a commanding voice. "You represent the culmination of more than a decade of research on behalf of Mastercorp. Why, I became involved in this program before some of you were born.

And now, here we are. You are Aniarmament—Mastercorp's most ferocious soldiers, our pack of cyborg attack animals. Now, sound off!"

The sickly boy stepped forward and flexed. The thousand knives of his metal wings spread like fan blades. "'Sup, lady? Name's Buzz. I'm the boss of Aniarmament and I provide air transport for the team with my boss wings."

"Let's get one thing straight, Buzz," Viola sneered. "The only boss around here is me. You are my field commander. Don't flatter yourself with a promotion I never granted."

"Sheesh, sure, lady, whatever." Buzz stepped back into line.

The girl did a standing front flip, landing in a crouch. She scraped her claws on the floor, creating a piercing sound that made Vesuvia's eyes water. The last time she heard a sound like that was at a True North boy band concert.

"I'm Kitty, ma'am," the girl with the cheetah legs said. "Speed and tactics are my specialties."

Last, the boy with the huge shell on his back lumbered forward. He sighed. "I'm Gregory. I'm a hermit crab. I'm the geek. And the muscle."

"Very good, Aniarmament. Now, your work begins." Viola pushed a button on the podium, illuminating a holographic projector. A 3-D image of a robot boy appeared before them. His jagged metal face framed crimson eyes that smoldered with hatred. His appearance was so hideous that Vesuvia gasped, but the children of Aniarmament appeared unfazed.

"Traitors of Mastercorp," the robot boy's mouth chomped like the jaw of a nutcracker. "Remember me? It is I, Benjamin Nagg, your former spy. You left me to die in your latest attack on the eighth continent, but you were only . . . mostly successful. Though the Anti-Eden Compound you so liberally sprinkled on the continent has changed my shape, I am still me. And I still have this!"

The hologram of Benjamin raised his metal gauntlet, revealing a single page of cyberpaper that read: *The Ultimate Continent Ownership Form. By every island and isthmus, by every archipelago, whosoever holds this document shall possess full ownership of THE 8TH CONTINENT.*

"Do you see, Mastercorp? Do you see, Viola, you severe crone? All your billions of dollars, all those underpaid employees who work so hard, it's all for nothing. This document says that I rule the eighth continent, and soon, everyone will know it. If you want the Ultimate Continent Ownership Form, come and get it! I'll be waiting."

The hologram of robot Benjamin vanished, leaving those in the cavernous docking bay in empty silence, as if a celebrity had just left a party and now the party was total lame sauce.

Viola cleared her throat. "Aniarmament, your job is to find this traitor and bring him back to our side for rehabilitation. At all costs you must retrieve the Ultimate Continent Ownership Form. The eighth continent must be ours. Our company sparked the creation of the Eden Compound that made this continent, and made you, as well. Demonstrate your gratitude with your obedience. Now go!"

The cyborg animal kids let loose bloody roars and raced to the end of the docking bay. The shark jaws at the front of the dreadnought opened. Kitty leaped onto the back of Gregory's shell. Buzz took to the air, grabbed Gregory's hands, and pulled his companions skyward. He soared between the dreadnought's teeth and disappeared into the sky below.

At last, Viola turned to face her daughter. "Come with me, Vesuvia."

She followed her mother to the bridge of the dreadnought, where Viola and Mister Dark could command all of Mastercorp's forces on the eighth continent. Vesuvia's head hurt, and the blinking lights on the dozen consoles circling the room didn't help. But her headache faded as she saw the front viewport. Sunlight. It felt so good on her face. She stepped closer, making sure to avoid a discolored patch of floor. Vesuvia could see where Mastercorp had repaired the gaping hole she had made with Anti-Eden Compound many months ago. She stared at the sky.

"Tell me, Vesuvia, have we seen the end of your tantrums? Your last outburst nearly destroyed the dreadnought and allowed our prisoner Evie Lane to escape."

"I am calm," Vesuvia answered, saying the words her mother wanted to hear, though the lies tasted sour in her mouth. "I know now that I made a terrible mistake, but it won't happen again. I hate Evie Lane. I hate her peppy energy and I hate her lies. I hate Rick Lane. I hate his know-it-all snobbery, and I hate his bossiness. I hate that whole family. Everything bad that has happened to me is their fault."

Her mother nodded approvingly. "And how do you feel about me?"

Vesuvia tasted bile in her mouth. "You are my wise mother. When I trust you and do as you say, things go well."

"Spoken like a true Mastercorp executive," her mother said. "I'm glad you have decided to rejoin us. I hope you understand that your long Time Out in that cell was for your own good. Now you will be of great help to the corporation. We have entered the final act, Vesuvia. Soon, an entire continent will be ours to do with as we please. The Mastercorp board of directors has been very clear in its instructions. We are to remove every trace of Winterpole from this continent and destroy that obnoxious Lane family. Once we have dealt with them, we can seize control of that eyesore of a city they rule."

Vesuvia turned to face her mother. "What do you mean, city?"

HIGH UP IN A TREESCRAPER, EVIE LANE STEPPED OUT ONTO A BRANCH AND LOOKED DOWN AT THE

continent hundreds of feet below. The sight of the stone huts and tall tree-shaped buildings made her heart swell. The rows of houses, restaurants, research facilities, and recreation hubs went on and on. The buildings merged with the natural landscape of the continent. They didn't have to cut anything down. In the lobbies of many buildings, trees grew up through the floor.

Evie couldn't believe that all their hard work had paid off at last. Finally, her family could share its new civilization—a society for fun, for creativity and science—with the world. The Lanes had won. Their city, officially named Scifun, was flourishing.

Six months ago this very spot had been the modest settlement of Evie's family, home only to a few worker robots and some enthusiastic scientists. Now, Scifun's population was approaching 100,000 people.

The wind whipped Evie's yellow T-shirt as she watched

her domain. Children raced through the streets with their tutors, laughing and learning. Lab technicians on a lunch break crowded a field where they played a live-action version of a popular real-time strategy computer game. One of Evie's best friends, the vegetarian cowboy Sprout Sanchez, led a group of newcomers on a guided tour through the city. One of Evie's big plans for the continent was to ensure that every new citizen received a warm welcome and a tour. She remembered how awkward it felt to start at a new school or move to a new place. She didn't want anyone to feel that way in Scifun.

From the high branch of the treescraper, Evie couldn't hear what Sprout was saying to the newcomers, but she was sure it was something about lassoing legumes or the corn corral he was building uptown at the foot of Mount Luck. Sprout's love of vegetables always made Evie giggle. She had never realized she could feel so much. The people of Scifun were a big family. She would do anything to protect them and this land they had created.

Khzzzt!—a hiss and crackle came over her pocket tablet. "Evie, could you come down here please?"

The voice on Evie's communicator belonged to her older brother, Rick. Now, Rick and Evie were an unstoppable team, but things hadn't always been so good between them. After a particularly nasty fight, she had even been convinced to attack the Lane settlement by none other than Vesuvia Piffle of Condo Corp. Or was it Mastercorp? She couldn't keep track.

Eventually, Evie realized she was wrong and came home to help her family rebuild. She was grateful that even after she had done such a terrible thing, Rick and the rest of her family had welcomed her home. Rick and Evie finally understood that the secret to success was compromise. Rick wanted to do scientific research. Evie wanted to have fun. They did both, and it worked—the progress their settlement had made was proof of that.

But sometimes, Evie woke up late at night shaking, fearful that she was still the Evie who had done the bad thing, who could never redeem her past mistakes. She knew she had much more to do to set things right.

Khzzzt! "Evie?"

"Coming, bro!" She leaped off the end of the tree branch and plummeted past a dozen windows. She fell, laughing giddily, as the wind blew her messy hair from her face.

The bungee cord started to stretch. *Boing!* Evie bobbed up and down, hanging by her feet from the sturdy tree branch. She peered into the open window of the treescraper beside her, which looked into Rick and their father's lab. "Hi!" Evie called out cheerfully.

Rick glanced up from his microscope and adjusted his glasses. When he saw her, he let out a sigh and shook his head, which made his poofy red hair wiggle. "Nice of you to drop in, Evie."

"I get it!" She said with a grin, swaying a bit as she dangled in the breeze. "That was like a pun or something. Very witty, Rick."

"Yes, thank you. I'm a riot." He walked to the window and picked up the big wooden shepherd's crook leaning against the wall. He used the end to hook Evie and pull her through the open window.

"Don't be so dry, son!" That was Dad, scientific genius and the Speaker of the Science Circle, a committee elected by Scifun's citizens. Evie, Rick, and their mother were also members of the Circle. Dad leaned against a car-sized computer terminal and smiled. "I thought your joke was genuinely witty, and you should never be afraid to be funny!"

"Thanks, Dad." Rick rubbed his cheeks. He looked tired.

"What's going on?" Evie nudged him. "What do you need?"

"Ah, right!" Rick cleared his throat. "Dad and I are in the middle of an important experiment. You know that gross residue in the ocean surrounding the continent?"

"Ew, yeah, it's super gross. That's like, the little bits of plastic left over from when the eighth continent was the Great Pacific Garbage Patch."

"Super correct, honey!" Dad again. He gave her a goofy grin. "2-Tor would be so proud of you."

Rick said, "Anyway, we're trying to find a way to get all that plastic out of the water. It's not easy, but so far our current experiment shows promise. We're trying to re-create the Eden Compound."

"That's right!" Dad said. "The Eden Compound would turn all that plastic into harmless organic matter."

"But I thought the formula for the Eden Compound

was lost when"—Evie swallowed, pushing a sad thought from her mind—"the Mastercorp research submarine was destroyed."

"It was!" Dad said cheerfully. "But we're gonna make up a new compound from scratch!"

Evie frowned. "Haven't you ever heard the expression *Don't reinvent the wheel*?"

Dad dismissed her with a wave of his hand. "Oh, that doesn't apply to this. We're trying to reinvent the whole car!"

With a laugh, Evie said, "Well, that's great! How can I help?"

Rick said, "Oh, no, we don't need your help with this. We're busy with our experiment, but I'm due for a meeting with Winterpole. Can you be my substitute today?"

"Ugh, Winterpole? But those guys are so boring!" Ever since the Lanes had made a truce with Mister Snow, the senior agent in charge of Winterpole's activities on the eighth continent, Evie had to admit that everything had been running more smoothly, in part because of the micromanaging bureaucracy Winterpole brought to the table. Law and order helped keep Scifun safe; although, Mister Snow's long ramblings on urban planning made Evie want to bring a pillow to committee meetings so she could sneak a power nap.

"I mean it, Rick. I can't take another two-hour lecture on hexagonal building formations."

"And why not?" asked a stern voice from the doorway. "Hexagonal building formations are *fascinating*."

Mister Snow stood at the entrance to the lab in his trim white suit, having arrived, as usual, at the worst possible moment. His dark hair appeared freshly cut, and his gray sideburns neatly buzzed.

Evie winced. "Oh, hey there, Mister Snow."

"Er, ahem," Dad said. "Very busy, yes, we're very busy." He scooted into his office. Rick followed. They shut the door, leaving Evie alone with the Winterpole agent.

But not for long.

"Don't take it personally, Mister Snow." Diana Maple came up the stairs behind her Winterpole supervisor. Diana was Evie's age, but she looked like she had drunk some of Professor Doran's supergrow serum because she had stretched four inches taller in the last two months. Now she towered over Evie, and her new agent uniform made her look smart and capable. Diana was so nice that when she sneezed, sugar and spice came out. Sometimes Evie couldn't believe a cool, friendly person like Diana could work for Winterpole, and even crazier, that she used to be best friends with Evie's archnemesis, Vesuvia Piffle. Either way, those days were over for Diana. No one had heard from Vesuvia in half a year, and Diana was one of the good guys.

Mister Snow's eyes moved between Evie and the closed door to her father's office. "We expected your brother to debrief us."

"Nope! Me today. Hey, Diana. What's up?"

"Hey, Evie." Diana waved. "Unfortunately, we have urgent news."

"It is so urgent I filled out three permission slips to move up our scheduled appointment and change its location," Mister Snow explained.

Diana nodded. "On a routine patrol, two of our agents made a startling discovery."

Evie raised an eyebrow. "What agents?"

From behind them, Evie heard more voices and footsteps coming up the stairs. "All I'm trying to say, Barry, is that hoverships shaped like enormous bumblebees are off-message for Winterpole."

"Quite the opposite, Larry. Bees represent cooperation and hard work—an excellent depiction of Winterpole's main objectives—while avoiding the usual links to snow and ice."

The two familiar agents Larry and Barry entered the lab. Diana chimed in. "I like it as a symbol. Winterpole gives us lots of busywork to do. That always makes me think of bees. You know, like a busy bee?"

"*You* are a busybody!" Barry snapped. He clutched his chest. "No one understands my mission to show the world just how wonderful Winterpole can be."

"I understand it," Larry said. "I just think it's dumb."

"Two penalties!" spat Barry. "Insulting a Winterpole agent."

"Knock it off, all of you." Mister Snow adjusted his necktie. "Proceed with your report."

Larry cleared his throat. "Barry and I just completed a perimeter sweep."

"That's right!" Barry added. "We circled the whole continent."

"And what did you find?" Evie asked.

"Bad news, I'm afraid," Diana said.

Mister Snow elaborated. "The agents sighted the Mastercorp dreadnought off the west coast of the continent, over by the ruins of New Miami."

Evie gulped. She had spent time imprisoned inside the giant black robo-shark and didn't envy anyone who caught a glimpse of it. "What was Mastercorp up to?"

"We don't know for sure," Mister Snow answered. "But I have submitted a request to Winterpole Headquarters that would allow me to speculate on the possibilities."

"You need permission for that?" Evie raised an eyebrow.

Mister Snow gave her a stern look. "Miss, at Winterpole you need permission for everything."

But Evie could speculate without permission just fine, and what she came up with wasn't comforting. Mastercorp had been trying to manufacture the Anti-Eden Compound, a substance that did the opposite of what the Eden Compound could do—it turned organic matter into inorganic materials like metal, plastic, and garbage. Mastercorp could be planning to turn the whole eighth continent back into a floating garbage patch.

"This is serious. Diana, please call an emergency meeting of the Science Circle," Evie said, worry creeping into her voice. "We have to figure out what to do about this news, before it's too late."

3

BENEATH SPIRE ONE, THE FIRST AND LARGEST TREESCRAPER IN SCIFUN, WHERE THE LANE FAMILY lived, was their personal storage vault. It was here that the Lanes kept their most treasured belongings, including everything recovered from the wreckage of Lane Mansion, which was destroyed in an unfortunate accident.

Rick had mixed feelings about going into the vault. The dark chamber was filled with happy memories of all the fun past experiments the family had conducted, like the hover pogo stick and the universal birdcall translator. (They had concluded that the translator didn't work, as it translated everything birds said as very bad words.) Many of the family treasures kept in the vault were broken or showed signs of serious damage from the accident. That accident had led to Rick's worst fight ever with Evie and it brought back bad memories of her time away from home. He didn't like thinking about that.

Rick knew the vault could also contain clues to re-creating the Eden Compound, so he reluctantly followed his father and sister through the vault, searching. After Evie had delivered Winterpole's report to the Science Circle, they held an emergency meeting to decide what to do about Mastercorp. They devised a multi-pronged strategy. Winterpole would handle security and monitor the dreadnought's movements. Meanwhile, Dad would continue trying to re-create the Eden Compound. He had invented that substance with Doctor Grant many years ago, and it had started Rick and Evie on their adventure to make the eighth continent in the first place. In case the unthinkable happened, and Mastercorp spilled Anti-Eden Compound all over the continent, a re-created Eden Compound would be the only way to reverse the effects.

The thought of Mastercorp harming even one person or one building in Scifun made Rick bristle. He and his family had done so much to create the eighth continent, and now with its survival at stake, he would do anything to protect it. He'd even promise never to play video games again if it meant the continent was safe. The continent was a symbol of all his hard work, and of his family being whole.

"What are we looking for, exactly?" Evie asked as they explored the vault.

Dad raised a flashlight and aimed the beam at dark corners of the room. "Lab notes, old hard drives, anything that might contain the formula for the Eden Compound."

Evie sighed. "But, Dad, you came up with the formula yourself. Why can't you just throw some ingredients together and guess?"

Rick rolled his eyes. "Really, Evie? That would be like Dad asking you to 'guess' the exact wording of an essay you wrote for school a year ago, and if you got one word, even one punctuation mark wrong, your essay would blow up in your face."

"Exploding homework? Cool!" Evie flashed Rick a mischievous grin.

Dad chuckled. "That reminds me of Poof Paper. One of my first inventions, when I was about your age, kids. If you did your homework on Poof Paper, and you were worried you weren't going to get the right answers, just fold in the corners and poof! The paper would disintegrate in a puff of smoke."

"But then you wouldn't have any answers at all!" Rick said.

Scratching his chin in thought, Dad said, "Hmm, well, I don't remember all the details. Hey, Evie. That reminds me. Go check out that filing cabinet over there."

Evie opened the dented cabinet. Peering into the top drawer she said, "Oh wow! Look how boring this is!"

"Come on, Rick," Dad said. "Follow me over here."

Rick tailed his father through the vault, until Dad stopped at an old steamer trunk covered in blankets. He pulled off the blankets and undid the clasps, then popped the trunk open. Inside was an assortment of dusty knickknacks.

"A lot of this stuff I haven't touched since college," Dad explained. "But that's a good thing. It means these are items untouched since I was a student working with Doctor Grant on the design of the Eden Compound."

Just the mention of Doctor Grant's name made Rick feel a pang in his chest. The good old doctor had heroically sacrificed himself to save Rick and Evie's lives and protect the Eden Compound, allowing them to create the eighth continent. Doctor Grant had taught Rick a lot about life and family and what it meant to be a good person.

"Oh hey, look at this!" Dad pulled a stack of framed pictures out of the trunk. He handed one to Rick. "Look like anyone you know?"

It was a photo of his father—he looked about ten years old in the picture—dressed as a cowboy. Sprout would have hooted and slapped his thigh if he had seen it. Young George Lane wore oversized glasses and sported the same dome of red hair that Rick had.

"And check this out." Dad held up another picture. In this photo, Dad was a teenager and wearing a mortarboard. It must have been his high school graduation. Standing beside him, with a proud arm around his son, was Rick's grandfather Jonas Lane.

Sort of. One of the sad truths Doctor Grant had told Rick aboard the Mastercorp research vessel the *Cichlid* was the secret of his father's upbringing. It had sparked the young George's lifelong obsession with cleaning up the planet.

Rick glanced over his shoulder. Evie had stuck her whole head inside the middle drawer of the filing cabinet and was pulling out a bunch of papers. She wasn't listening. Maybe now was the time to ask the question. Rick had been too afraid to ask all this time, out of fear of—he wasn't sure, exactly—the answer? With Mastercorp back after them and Doctor Grant on his mind, he could no longer keep the question inside.

"Dad . . . Who were my grandparents?"

Rick's father stopped still. He did not look up from the trunk as he asked, "What do you mean, son?"

"Doctor Grant . . . He told me about the garbage dump. About the orphanage. How Grandpa"—Rick lowered his voice—"adopted you."

"I see." Dad usually had such a goofy expression on his face, always trying to crack a joke and make Rick laugh. Now he had a somber look, deep in thought, or perhaps just sad. "I don't know, Richard. Nobody knew, and perhaps we never will."

"But with all your success and money, didn't you ever wonder who your parents were? Didn't you ever think to go looking?"

"Of course I did! So many times. But you can't buy the answers to life's mysteries, son. For a long time I was consumed with the desire to know who my parents were. It's the question humans have been puzzling since the beginning of time: Where did I come from? I searched. I researched. I pushed my brain to its limit, yet I never found out who my parents were. And you know what? That's okay. Because it doesn't matter who they were. Jonas Lane was my father, and I'm your father, and you will never be alone. That is what matters."

Rick's eyes felt moist, but before he could react his dad pulled him into a deep hug. When at last they parted, Rick glanced down and noticed another picture frame in the steamer trunk.

"Hey, what's this?" he asked, picking up the photo. The glass was cracked. "Must have been damaged in the crash."

The photo was a picture of Dad with Doctor Grant. The old doctor had a big grin on his face, the same grin he'd had when Rick and Evie had helped him complete the Eden Compound, over a year ago. Had it been that long?

As Rick contemplated this, the back of the damaged picture frame fell off and landed on the floor with a crash.

Evie gasped. "What the heck was that?"

"I'm sorry, Dad." Rick said. But his father wasn't listening; he was staring intently at the piece of the frame still in Rick's hand. Rick looked down at it. "What?"

Turning over the frame, Rick saw something written on the back of the photo in black marker.

"I didn't know that was there," Dad said. "That's Doctor Grant's handwriting."

Rick squinted at the messy script. "To learn my secrets, just ask my friend from Copenhagen." He looked up, puzzled. "Copenhagen? Did Doctor Grant work with any scientists from Denmark?"

Evie squealed. "Wait! Wait! I know the answer. I remember this from one of 2-Tor's quizzes."

Rick did not like the idea that his little, easily distracted sister had solved a brainteaser before him, but he was stumped. "Okay, who is it?"

Breathlessly, Evie said, "A famous scientist, from Copenhagen. It's Niels Bohr!"

"But he died in 1962," Rick said.

"Not that Niels Bohr!"

It felt like Rick's brain was a house and someone had run through turning on all the lights. "Doctor Grant's cat! Niels Bohr! Of course! How could I be so dumb?"

"It's a mystery," Evie grinned. "We have to find that cat. Come on!"

BENJAMIN NAGG HELD HIS CLAWED, METAL HAND UP IN THE AIR. NARROW BEAMS OF SUNLIGHT

pierced the tree canopy, reflecting off the gleaming surface of his artificial paw. It was quiet in the forest. The wind whispered through the trees. A freshwater brook murmured nearby. Inside Benjamin's head, a voice was screaming.

ANGLE EXTREMITY JOINTS. READY COMBAT POSITION. SUBDUE EMOTIVATORS. STAND BY. STAND BY.

Benjamin clenched his robotic hand in a tight fist, ready to strike anything that came close. He was so filled with vengeful fury that he wondered if his metal skull would melt.

AIRBORNE INTRUDERS DETECTED. INITIATE INTENTION SPECULATION. ANALYSIS COMMENCING IN THREE . . . TWO . . . ONE . . .

Intruders? Benjamin's microphonic ears had not heard anything. His eyes, which had been transformed by the Anti-Eden Compound into high-definition cameras, could only see the slightest traces of infrared light through the treetops. The roboticized boy ran between two trees and ducked into his cave, the hideout where he had been concealing himself for months from the Lanes, Winterpole, and Mastercorp. His metal hands grabbed the camouflage door, an eight-foot square panel woven from branches he had stripped off nearby trees. He covered the entrance to the cave. Then Benjamin peered through the leaves, waiting for the intruders.

His sensors picked up the sound of flapping metal wings. He recorded the *ting* sound they made and processed the audio in his databanks.

AUDIO FILE IDENTIFIED: LIGHTWEIGHT ALUMINUM SEGMENTS. PROBABILITY 91.9%.

Seconds later, Benjamin saw the source of the sound. Three kids dropped out of the sky and planted their feet in the dirt. They had robotic enhancements that gave each a strong resemblance to a different animal. One was a scrawny punk kid with a shaved head and a nose ring. He looked like one of the kids who rode a skateboard and used to pick on Benjamin back when he was human.

The boy wore a leather collar around his neck and a black T-shirt with a white skull on it. His T-shirt had two slits running down the back, and emerging from those openings were ten-foot-long aluminum wings. The sound of the massive wings flapping was what Benjamin's sensors had picked up. The serrated feathers looked sharp enough to sever bone. He was a human buzzard.

The two other kids looked equally bizarre. There was

a nimble girl with the legs of a cheetah, and she pounced around the wooded glade, sniffing the air and looking for something—Benjamin, no doubt. The third and final member of this ridiculous zoo was a tiny boy wearing glasses half the size of his face. A huge shell covered his back, like that of a giant hermit crab.

Buzzard Kid slapped the back of Crab Boy's shell, which was covered in engraved swirls and gentle peaks. "Open up, Gregory. Let's get the scanners running."

"I hate when you do that, Buzz."

Gregory grumbled as he crouched down on his hands and knees so that Buzz could pop open a compartment on the back of his shell. It revealed a laptop computer and a small satellite dish. The dish spun in a lazy circle, and when Buzz opened the computer, Benjamin used his telescopic vision to examine the screen. It looked like radar of the area. Little red dots represented the life signatures of his three enemies.

He knew what they were after. Benjamin opened the small storage compartment on his left thigh and reached inside. He caressed the Ultimate Continent Ownership Form with his hand.

"I can't figure out what these little dots mean," Buzz growled.

"Bring it over here," Gregory said. Buzz removed the laptop from his shell and brought it to the bespectacled boy. Gregory examined the data. "Okay, Buzz, look at this. These little dots are us. Three members of Aniarmament, three life signatures. There's you and me next to each other. And that one off away from the others must be Kitty."

The girl with the cheetah legs was standing a foot behind them. "What are you talking about? I'm right here."

The boys looked over at her, then back at the screen. "Hmm . . ." Gregory squinted. "Oh, I see. This large dot is actually two conjoined dots, representing Buzz and my combined signatures."

"Then who is that fourth dot?" Buzz asked.

WARNING. HOSTILE ACTION DETECTED. INITIATE EVASION PROTOCOL.

Alarms quite literally went off inside Benjamin's head. But before he could react, a robotic claw at the end of a long metal arm emerged from a flap in Gregory's cyber shell. It shot across the glade and burst through the leafy panel covering Benjamin's cave. The claw grasped him around the throat and ripped him through the leaves.

Twigs snapped. The panel broke with a crack. The claw dragged Benjamin into the clearing. Benjamin grabbed the metal arm. With an intense burst of strength, he tore the claw off him.

"Ow! Ow!" Gregory wailed, retracting the claw into his shell.

Buzz and Kitty tensed their cybernetic enhancements and tackled Benjamin.

RELEASE DEFENSIVE MEASURES. COUNTER-ATTACK. INCREASE TORQUE.

Benjamin extended his fists and rotated three hundred

and sixty degrees, swiveling around his waist. His outstretched arms acted like a tornado, knocking Buzz away. Kitty leaped onto Benjamin's back, but the robot boy grabbed her and threw her against Gregory's shell. There was a loud *dong* as she struck the shell, and Kitty and Gregory rolled across the ground.

"How dare Viola send such weaklings against me!?" Benjamin let out a digitized growl. "Are you the best Mastercorp has to offer? How amusing!"

"She's the boss. We're going to do as she asks." Buzz wiped blood from his nose.

"I am the ruler of this continent," Benjamin said. "Me. I am your king. Your nightmare. You cannot defeat me."

"We're not here to defeat you," Gregory groaned, flopping, his face in the dirt with his big shell weighing him down. "We're here to get you to join us. We want you on our team."

"That's right," Buzz said, slowly approaching Benjamin. "Mastercorp needs you. You know about the Lane city, right? Scifun? We need to destroy it. And Winterpole too. Mastercorp wants us to take them out, with your ownership form, and with your great power."

"Don't you remember all the good times you had working for Mastercorp?" Kitty asked. "Betraying Winterpole as a double agent?"

ANALYZING PROBABILITIES. CALCULATING OUTCOMES. EVALUATING COMBATANT SKILL SETS.

The robotic words burned in Benjamin's head.

"Mastercorp left me to die in the ruins of New Miami!"

"But you didn't die, did you?" Buzz flapped his metal wings. "And now look at you. Look how powerful you are. Just like us."

"You're right," Benjamin said as he flexed his metal hand. "I am strong, thanks to Mastercorp's actions. I will join you brats, but I will be your leader. The leader of the Brat Brigade."

Buzz, Kitty, and Gregory knelt before Benjamin.

"As long as you serve Mastercorp, we are your loyal brats," Buzz said.

Benjamin nodded in satisfaction. "Excellent. And our first task will be to use the UCOF and seize control of the eighth continent!"

ATOP A HILL ALONG THE SOUTHERN COAST OF THE EIGHTH CONTINENT, PAST THE WESTERN EDGE OF

Scifun, a humble stone marker emerged from the tall grass, facing the sea. Evie took a deep breath when she saw the stone.

They could have flown the *Roost* to the hill in just a few minutes, but Evie wanted to walk. It was a sunny and breezy day, and the ocean made such lovely noises as it danced across the beach.

Rick walked at Evie's side, and Sprout joined them. 2-Tor took up the rear, his metal joints squeaking as he followed the children. The eight-foot-tall mechanical crow had been quiet since he and Evie escaped from the Mastercorp dreadnought. Evie suspected he missed Didi, Vesuvia's tutor and fellow robo-bird. The two had formed a close bond. Evie couldn't even remember the last time he had administered a quiz.

"Hey, 2-Tor," Evie said. "How come you never quiz us any more? Algebra! Evie has twice as many continents as Rick. Rick has three continents, plus an unknown number of continents—let's call it X continents. If Evie has eight continents, then what is the unknown number?"

"X equals one!" Rick said breathlessly as he reached the top of the grassy hill.

"I was asking 2-Tor," Evie said.

"Oh, Miss Evelyn," 2-Tor said admiringly. "It defragments my internal drives to see you demonstrate such a strong comprehension of mathematics."

Evie smiled, glad to brighten her robot friend's mood. "Of course, you silly bird. After everything we've been through, it shouldn't be a surprise that *something* you said rubbed off on me."

Sprout tipped back his cowboy hat and wiped his brow with a handkerchief. "I don't get it. If Evie has eight continents, then how can Rick have continents too? Are there more than eight continents? And how do you 'have' continents in the first place? I reckon Evie ain't telling us the whole story."

"Yee-haw! I always tell the truth." Evie leaped onto Sprout's back. He took off like a rocket, and soon they joined Rick on top of the hill. They collapsed onto the grass in a fit of giggles. As 2-Tor joined them on the summit, Evie noticed the sad expression on Rick's face. She followed his eyes to the stone marker facing the sea.

DOCTOR EVAN GRANT

Inventor

Mentor

Friend

Evie's heart twisted up in a knot. She had not been

prepared for her return to Doctor Grant's memorial to be so emotional, but it didn't surprise her. Doctor Grant had been a giving teacher to Rick and Evie *and* their father. He sacrificed himself to save Evie's life and made the eighth continent a reality.

Rick stared at his feet. "We haven't been up here much lately. Things have been so busy in Scifun."

Evie put her arm around his shoulders. "I know. I feel bad, but I think he would be happy that we're busy."

"Do not feel sorrow, children," 2-Tor soothed them. "The doctor has not been totally alone."

"*Rrrrowl!*" A lanky orange cat slinked around the side of the stone memorial. He purred loudly at the sight of Rick and Evie.

"Niels Bohr!" Evie ran to the cat and scooped him up in her arms. The cat nuzzled her cheek and dug his claws into her shirt. Evie winced. Cats had weird ways of showing affection.

Evie carried him over to the others. When 2-Tor reached out a wing tip to pet the cat's fur, Niels Bohr pounced onto 2-Tor's shoulder and climbed onto the robo-bird's beak. The cat let his tail and paws dangle off the sides, considering the beak an acceptable place to sleep.

"I say, children, this is most uncomfortable." 2-Tor's voice was muffled thanks to the cat napping on his beak. Niels Bohr meowed irritably, as if he considered it quite rude for 2-Tor to disturb him.

Evie suppressed a giggle. Niels Bohr had been living out

here by the memorial ever since the garbage patch had become the eighth continent. Every few days someone would spot him padding around the settlement looking for food. Mostly he stayed close to his former owner. He must have been happy to see his old friends.

"All right," Sprout said, looking around the group. "So we found the tiger cat. 'My friend from Copenhagen,' as y'all were saying. Now what?"

"Good question," Evie answered. "How is a cat supposed to help us figure out how to re-create the Eden Compound?"

Niels Bohr purred lazily. His whiskers twitched into a little cat smile, almost as if he knew the answer.

Rick scratched his chin. "I'm not sure how he's going to help us, but I believe the note Doctor Grant left behind has to be a clue."

Evie sighed. "Even if Niels Bohr did know Doctor Grant's secrets, how could he tell us? He's just a cat."

Niels Bohr meowed aggressively, as if he took great offense at being called "just a cat."

"Maybe there's a secret message hidden in his collar," Rick offered.

Evie looked through the fur on Niels Bohr's neck, but he wasn't wearing a collar. She gave him a pat on the head. "Come on, little guy. Give us a hint."

The cat hopped off 2-Tor's beak. "My word!" The robot moaned. Niels Bohr curled up at Evie's feet, showing off the silky fur and dark stripes along his back. He rubbed back and forth across Evie's legs until his fur was ruffled in such a way that you could see down to the mottled skin underneath. Evie squinted at it. There were markings on Niels Bohr's skin, markings she had never seen before. She supposed she had never really looked that closely. The markings looked almost like . . .

"Hey, Rick, check this out!" Evie spread the fur apart. Rick and Sprout crowded over the cat. "What is this, like a tattoo?"

"It's writing," Rick said. "See? That's a letter 'A.' But I can't read it. The fur is too thick."

"Who would tattoo a cat?" Sprout asked, puzzled.

"I don't know," Evie said. "But it seems like a good way to hide a secret message."

"So how do we read it?" Rick asked.

"We'll have to shave his fur, I guess," Evie said. "Then it'll be clear to read the message."

Niels Bohr meowed in displeasure.

"I mean, come on!" Evie offered the boys a weak grin. "How hard could it be to shave a cat?"

Bottles of soap and jars of face cream clattered to the floor as Niels Bohr scrambled across the shelf in Evie's mother's bathroom. Half-coated in shaving cream, Niels Bohr meowed hysterically, leaping from the shelf to the sink, the sink to the tile floor.

"He's squirmier than a worm in an apple!" Sprout

observed. The cat twisted and writhed on the tiles, trying to kick the shaving cream off his fur with a paw.

Rick laughed. "That's a nice way of putting it."

"My word!" 2-Tor wailed. "What will Missus Lane say?"

Evie looked down at the razor and can of shaving cream in her hands. They'd been at this for two hours since returning to the Lane family's private apartment in Spire One, and they were no closer to reading the secret message tattooed on Niels Bohr's skin. Mom was going to throw a fit when she saw what a mess they had made.

Niels Bohr hissed at the pile of shaving cream he had kicked onto the floor.

"I told you the cream was a bad idea," Rick said. "Maybe we should try the clippers again." He switched on the electric clippers in his hand. They buzzed loudly. The sound sent the tiger cat into another tizzy. He jumped five feet into the air and landed in the empty bathtub.

"Please, Niels Bohr!" Evie begged. "We need your help. I know it's unpleasant, but we really need to read that message. You're our only hope at stopping Mastercorp. We need to know what Doctor Grant left for us. We can't do it without you."

At his former owner's name, Niels Bohr poked his head over the edge of the tub. He squinted at Evie, folded back his ears, and said *"Rrrowl!"*

"Please . . ." Evie stepped closer. When the cat didn't move, she set down the razor and shaving cream and petted the cat's head. "Help us."

Niels Bohr purred and nuzzled her hand, and then he walked in a tight circle on the floor of the tub and laid down, exposing the patch of his back where the tattoo was. Evie waved Rick over, and as the buzzing clippers came closer, Niels Bohr covered his face with his front paws.

A few furry moments later, Evie was cradling a skinny, hairless tiger cat in her arms, and Rick was scooping vast quantities of fur into a canvas sack for repurposing. The cat watched mournfully as the fur disappeared.

"Don't worry, little guy." Evie gave Niels Bohr a soothing hug. "It'll grow back.

They crowded around the cat and examined the markings on his skin. There were two lines of text. Sprout tried to decipher the first line. "Colon-Slash-Slash . . . What does this mean?"

"Looks like a uniform resource locator," Rick said.

"A URL?" Evie examined the text. "Like for a website?"

Rick pulled out his pocket tablet and typed in the address. White text on a plain black background appeared. ENTER PASSWORD, it said.

"Maybe this is the code," Evie said, pointing at the second line of the tattoo. It looked like a random string of letters, numbers, and symbols, but maybe it wasn't so random.

Rick typed it in and then the screen changed. The glow of the screen illuminated the children's faces. Niels Bohr meowed in surprise. Evie couldn't believe what she saw.

DIANA CLIPPED HER OFFICIAL WINTERPOLE ICE CLEATS ONTO THE SOLES OF HER SHOES AND stepped out of the hover-shuttle onto the north coast of the eighth continent. She wished she could have stayed in Scifun to help her friends stave off Mastercorp's advances on the island. But Winterpole had a great deal of work to do, and the Winterpole outpost was where she was needed most.

A troop of guards in iceberg helmets tromped across the frozen ground. Most of the base was comprised of the network of winding tunnels beneath them, but the launchpad for all airborne missions was up on the surface, and those vehicles had to be guarded.

Agents Barry and Larry slipped and slid over to the elevator tube that would take them down to the base's main chamber underground. Diana stayed close to Mister Snow, who walked with purpose to the communications relay on the western end of the frozen launchpad. Unlike Barry and Larry, Mister Snow had remembered his ice cleats.

He waved her over to the satellite dish where the communications agent was printing a list of messages from a mechanical typewriter. Mister Snow tore off the first several messages for examination.

Diana found it funny that she and Mister Snow had done so much work together the past six months. When she first began training as a junior agent, she had thought Mister Snow was totally the bad guy, but ever since she had convinced him to forge an alliance with the Lanes, they had transformed this base into the most productive Winterpole outpost on the planet. After Benjamin Nagg had been exposed as a double agent secretly working for Mastercorp, Snow had appointed Diana as Special Agent in Charge of Modernization and Efficiency, which was a fancy way of saying that she helped the base avoid unnecessary paperwork and loosened some of the absurd, restrictive rules for which Winterpole was famous. The end result: agents on the eighth continent worked less and accomplished more.

Mister Snow glanced up from the typed messages and shook his head at her. "This is very bad news."

"We work for Winterpole. It's always bad news." Diana gave him a reassuring smile. "What's wrong now?"

"Your mother is coming."

"My . . . mother?"

Diana felt as if a black hole large enough to swallow the sun had opened under her feet and consumed her.

Mrs. Maple was Winterpole's senior agent in charge of

enforcement, one of the highest-ranking officers in the entire organization. If she was coming to the eighth continent, something was not only very wrong; it meant something had to be *enforced*.

The roar of a hundred hover engines struck Diana's ears. She looked to the sky and saw a vast fleet of Winterpole airships coming in for a landing.

"Well, they don't waste any time, do they?" Diana sighed. This was not going to be good.

The lead hovership, the largest of the armada, was bluish white and shaped like an enormous icicle. The engines flared and the ship plummeted toward the surface like it was going to pierce the ground. The ship pulled up at the last second and slid to a stop only meters from where Diana and Mister Snow stood.

A metal hatch opened in the side of the icicle and Diana's mother emerged. Her Winterpole uniform was so sharply tailored, laundered so crisply, it looked like her clothes were frozen. Her hair was perfectly straight and cut at a severe angle, like axe blades along her jaw. With keen blue eyes she studied the structures that dotted the launchpad, the elevator tubes, and the Winterpole agents patrolling the area.

Behind her, a silver dome exited the giant icicle. The four big wheels under the dome were wrapped in snow chains. Helmeted agents steered the dome toward the largest elevator tube.

"We're moving the Director's isolation chamber to the

sub-levels of this compound. Mister Snow, effective immediately, you are relieved of command. Hello, Diana."

It was almost too much information for Diana to process all at once. What was the Director of Winterpole doing here, and why was he hiding inside a silver dome? Weird. And now Mister Snow wasn't in charge of the outpost?

"Mom, you can't transfer Mister Snow. We've done incredible things with this outpost. We're doing good work, and there is a lot at stake now. You have to see that."

"What I see is that you have allied with a known rule breaker and terrorist, George Lane, and his family," Mrs. Maple said sternly. "This outpost is an aberration and it must be returned to our standard protocols. You are operating in violation of three hundred Winterpole regulations."

Diana interrupted. "You don't understand. Let me show you how much we have accomplished here. I think you'll be impressed with—"

"No, *you* don't understand." Diana's mother straightened her uniform. "My opinion on the matter is completely irrelevant. Winterpole's rules *must* be followed. Unfortunately for everyone involved, your actions here have labeled you both as traitors."

Mister Snow sputtered, "But that can't be right. I've always been so careful to work within the boundaries of Winterpole's rules."

"I'm sorry, Diana, but I didn't make the rules." Mrs. Maple snapped her fingers and a squad of guards surrounded Diana and Mister Snow. Mrs. Maple said, "Your new duty is to serve as guides and ambassadors to my agents. Show us all the modernizations you have committed, so we can undo them. You will get my people up to speed, so that we may run this outpost at a level of efficiency appropriate for Winterpole. Show them where the bathrooms are. That's your job now. Your only job. And I don't want to hear a single complaint, young lady."

The guards marched Diana and Mister Snow to the nearest elevator tube. One of them leaned over to Diana. "So, uh, hey. Which way do you go to get to the mess hall from here? I'm starving!"

AN UNFORESEEN MUTATION OF PROFESSOR DORAN'S HOLLOW TREES, WHICH HAD GROWN TO

tremendous size and become the buildings that comprised a majority of Scifun's skyline, was that they blossomed. Bright-pink flowers and thick green leaves bloomed across the upper canopy of the hollow trees. It was in this fragrant, colorful tent of flora that the Science Circle held their meetings. Rick had issued an emergency alert to all members that he, along with Evie, Sprout, 2-Tor, and of course Niels Bohr, had made an important discovery. The eighth continent's ruling body had to rendezvous in the Circle's meeting room as soon as possible.

Nearly an hour had passed since the meeting was scheduled to begin, but there was still no sign of Mister Snow or Diana Maple and they hadn't answered any of his messages. Something was wrong. Rick could feel it. Winterpole agents were always punctual, and Diana never ignored his messages. But there was nothing he could do about it now.

"Time is short," Rick said. "We must start the meeting. Apologies to absent friends." The missing agents gave him a stomachache, but what he said was true. Time *was* short.

He looked around the circle. Wooden benches encircled the roof of Spire Two. Rick sat in the center of the circle on a chair carved from the top of the great hollow tree. The chair spun to face any member of the Science Circle. The members of the circle watched Rick with anticipation, waiting for him to speak.

"What's all this about, son?" Rick's father asked.

"Earlier today, Evie, Sprout, 2-Tor, and I investigated the clue we found in the family vault. In the end we uncovered a secret code tattooed on Doctor Grant's old cat, Niels Bohr."

From Evie's lap, Niels Bohr meowed an objection.

"Doctor Grant's old *tiger* cat. Sorry, Niels Bohr." Rick adjusted his glasses. "We found an encrypted website Doctor Grant had set up before his death, which provided us with information about the location of his lab notes. We believe these notes have the data we need to re-create the Eden Compound."

"So where are they?" Dad asked eagerly.

"On the Mastercorp research vessel the *Cichlid*."

"The submarine where we created the Eden Compound the first time," Evie added. "Where Doctor Grant was kept prisoner. Where he . . ."

Rick frowned as she trailed off, feeling his sister's sorrow. "Doctor Grant hid something on that submarine. His encrypted website clearly says so. We need to send someone to the wreckage of the sub and collect whatever he hid there."

There was a cold silence. A light breeze rustled the plants above their heads.

"We should send a soldier," suggested the Representative of Security.

No," replied the Secretary of Energy, an old college pal of Rick's parents. "It should be a scientist! Someone who understands the good doctor's sophisticated scientific notes."

"You're both wrong." The skinny teenager to Rick's left raised his rose-tinted sunglasses and winked at Rick. Tristan Ruby said, "It should be someone who carries the voice of the people. Like me!"

"I volunteer," Evie said in a soft voice. "I want to go. I owe it to everyone . . . to Doctor Grant."

The group went quiet. Rick could tell that they knew Evie was right. It had to be her. She knew the layout of the sub. She knew where it had sunk. Most of all, she knew that this was her chance at redemption, her way of making up for everything that happened when she and Vesuvia had attacked the eighth continent.

"I'll go too," Sprout said suddenly, rising from his seat. His cowboy hat fell off his lap and onto the floor. "I'm going crazy as a veggie stir-fry with nothing to do around here. I'll help you on your mission, Evie, if you'll have me."

"Of course I'll have you, Sprout!" Evie gave him a big smile. "Let's dust off the *Roost* and get moving. There isn't a moment to lose."

Rick stood on Scifun Airport's runway, watching one of Sprout's robots, a carrying carrot, load the *Roost* with supplies. His old beloved hovership had seen better days. They'd flown all over the world and had many adventures, but ever since tugging the eighth continent across the Pacific last year, the *Roost*'s controls had been clunky and the hover engine sputtered, like a grumpy old relative who always complains and never leaves the house.

Evie clapped her brother on the back. "Good luck, Rick. Don't get into too much trouble without me."

Rick grimaced. While they were gone, he would be scrambling to ready Scifun's defenses and continue his work trying to re-create the Eden Compound, not to mention find out what happened to Diana and Mister Snow. Still, it wasn't as scary or dangerous as the task that lay before Sprout and Evie. "I'm the one who should be wishing you luck. Be careful out there."

"We'll be back so fast you won't even miss us. Don't worry. You'll have the Eden Compound before you know it."

"I wish I was going with you."

"The continent needs you," she said. "Mastercorp could try to pull some funny business any second."

Rick nodded. She was right, of course. His sister gave him one last smile and hurried aboard the *Roost*. Then Sprout approached Rick. He was wringing his hat in his hands and had an awkward look on his face.

"Well, I guess this is so long for a while," Sprout said. "But I'm gonna look after Evie. I promise."

Rick had a funny feeling in his stomach, like maybe this was goodbye. Not for a while. Forever.

"Please be careful, Sprout," Rick pleaded.

"Aw, heck, Rick. I'll be as careful as I cook cauliflower."

"Listen," Rick said, knowing that this was the time to say what he felt. "You've always been such a good friend to me, Sprout. I want you to know how much I appreciate that. You make me feel like I'm cool, and that means a lot to me."

"Well, shoot. That's a mighty fine thing of you to say. The truth is, I never did none of that stuff. You are cool, Rick. Super cool. If you feel that way because of me, it's only because I think it's true."

Sprout Sanchez hugged Rick, then turned and disappeared into the *Roost*. The hover engine flared. The great tree rocketed high into the air and took off north over the continent. With a sinking feeling in his stomach, Rick stood on the runway, watching the tiny splinter in the sky, until it disappeared over the horizon.

BZZZT! **THE EXPOSED CIRCUIT BOARD VESUVIA WAS WORKING ON SPARKED, ZAPPING HER WITH** an unpleasant number of volts.

"Owie ow ow! Didi!" Vesuvia whined. "Didi, why don't you stop being the laziest robot on the planet and do this work for me?"

The bright-pink robo-bird clacked her plastic beak haughtily. "Vesuvia Piffle, if you were not the creator of my robot body, I swear, I would squish you like a little blond bug."

Vesuvia huffed. She flopped onto her back and looked up at the ceiling. Her mother had dumped her in the dreadnought's machine shop for hard labor. Everything was terrible, as usual. Her days were filled with rewiring, debugging, and boredom. She had been tasked with perfecting a dispersal mechanism for the Anti-Eden Compound bombs. She couldn't remember the last time she had a spa day. The actual work was fun. Vesuvia enjoyed tinkering with her little robots, but being locked in the workshop was as bad as being back in Time Out. Worse, her pink dress was covered in dark grease and burn marks from the sparks of her soldering iron.

"What's wrong, Vesuvia?" Didi pecked around the workshop, picking up discarded pink lemonade juice boxes and strawberry-shortcake-flavored ice cream cartons, which had comprised the majority of Vesuvia's diet lately.

"Oh not much, just *everything*, Didi." Vesuvia sighed. "Mom's going to take over the world, and here I am doing the work of a peasant!"

"But you're doing a good job, Vesuvia." Didi flapped her wings. "It's actually nice to see you accomplish something for a change, even if you do whine about it the whole time."

A harsh mechanical sound hit Vesuvia's ears as she heard someone unlock and open the door to the machine shop. Mister Dark stepped into the room. "Piffle. Your mother demands your presence."

"Ugh, now what?" Vesuvia sat up in annoyance.

Mister Dark's biceps bulged against the sleeves of his suit coat. "Clearly you have confused yourself with someone who gets to ask questions."

With one of her patented huffy sighs, Vesuvia followed the Mastercorp agent through the dreadnought, up to the top level. In a deserted corridor they came upon a ladder that led up to a circular hatch.

"Your mother is on the observation deck," Mister Dark told Vesuvia, pointing at the hatch. "I'll be here when you finish, assuming she doesn't throw you off the top of the dreadnought."

"Ha ha, very funny," Vesuvia sneered.

Mister Dark narrowed his eyes. "Did I make a joke?"

Shaken, Vesuvia climbed the ladder and with great strain opened the hatch. She pulled herself up onto the observation deck, a small platform overlooking the black metal expanse of the Mastercorp hovership. The roaring wind whipped Vesuvia's blond curls.

Her mother stood at the far end of the observation deck. She was talking to a hologram of a giant head floating in the air. It was the head of a middle-aged man with thinning, slicked-back gray-white hair and an impressive fake tan that made his skin look almost orange.

"Everyone on the board is very proud of the work you're doing, Viola," said the giant head.

"Thank you, sir." Vesuvia's mother clasped her hands behind her back and bowed to the head. "That means a great deal coming from the CEO of Mastercorp."

"How goes the development of the Anti-Eden Compound bombs?"

"Exceptionally well, sir. We are on target to make our deadline."

"Good! And what of this memo I received about the Lanes trying to re-create the original Eden Compound formula? Their success would be a massive setback for us."

"I have a meeting to discuss appropriate counter-measures as soon as our conversation is over, sir."

"Excellent. We are past the point of subtlety, Viola. If any of the Lanes get in the way, kill them."

Vesuvia swallowed nervously.

Viola hesitated. "Kill them, sir?"

"I do not repeat orders." When the head spoke, its mouth opened so wide Vesuvia thought the hologram might swallow her mother whole. "Send another report as soon as the bombs are ready."

"Yes, sir." Viola bowed to the head as it shrank into a beam of light and vanished inside the holographic projector.

A wicked scowl crossed Viola's face as she turned and spotted her daughter. "Speak not a word of that to anyone. It's classified information. Understand?"

Vesuvia twirled a lock of her hair around her finger. "Yeah, sure. Whatever."

"Not whatever!" Viola raised her hands. The red light on her bracelet flashed, and suddenly a flock of black mechanical ravens swooped out of the sky. They landed on the metal railing that surrounded the observation deck and clutched the metal in their sharp talons. The caws and shrieks of the birds made Vesuvia cover her ears in pain. "You think this is a game, Vesuvia? You will obey me!"

Viola pointed a finger at Vesuvia. The light on her bracelet flashed again. The red eyes of the mechanical ravens flashed the same way. The birds took flight and swarmed Vesuvia, grasping at her dress with their talons and pecking her.

"Ow! Yuck! Get these flying rats off me!"

The birds beat their wings against the air, plucking Vesuvia off the ground. They pulled her over the railing and away from the observation deck. Vesuvia screamed. Far below she could see the ocean and the eighth continent in the distance. They were thousands of feet in the air.

"Let me go! Let me go!" Vesuvia pleaded.

"They'll let you go right into the ocean if you don't shut up," Viola said viciously. "Now, will you continue mouthing off to your dear sweet mother?"

"Yes! I mean, no, I won't continue. Please put me down!"

The bracelet flashed, and the birds returned Vesuvia to the deck. As she landed, she felt all the blood in her body rush to her legs. Her hands shook. She looked up at her mother with confusion and disgust. Viola had never exactly been a loving mother, but this was a side of her that Vesuvia had never seen before.

Viola continued the conversation as if nothing had happened. "Vesuvia, child, why don't you see that I'm trying to help you by discouraging your bratty behavior? I'm doing what's best for us."

"What's best for us?" Vesuvia shuddered.

"Yes. Once we control the eighth continent, we won't need Mastercorp anymore. I will rule this world as queen. And you, my sweet girl, will be my princess. Once you learn to listen to your mother and do everything I say."

Vesuvia felt her brain being pulled in two. Seconds ago her mother had nearly killed her, and now she was offering her a throne.

"Didi will continue your work on the bomb dispenser. I have a new job for you."

"A . . . j-job?" Vesuvia asked.

"Yes," Viola said. "You and Mister Dark are going to murder Evie Lane."

9

THE BOTTOM OF THE OCEAN WAS LIKE AN ALIEN WORLD. CRAGGY MUCK STRETCHED INTO A HAZE of blue clouds as far as Evie's headlamp could reach. She'd heard that creepy fish hunted in this part of the ocean, fish and assorted gelatinous wildlife, but she wouldn't let herself be scared.

"*Meow!*" The purr came over the short-range communicator in Evie's dive helmet. She glanced over. Niels Bohr swam beside her, wearing a four-legged pressurized wetsuit and a dive helmet with little domes for his kitty ears.

"Hey, Evie, do you reckon we're close?" On her other side, Sprout swam in a similar outfit, minus the ear domes.

"Yeah, Sprout, I think we're almost there."

They had used the *Roost*'s tracking systems to find the wreckage of the Mastercorp research vessel the *Cichlid*. The pressure suits and weighted dive boots had hurried them to the ocean floor. Now that they were here, they had to find the submarine.

Niels Bohr kicked ahead, swimming as gracefully as a

bald cat in a rubber suit. He had been a last-minute addition to their team. Evie didn't know why Niels Bohr would want to go back into frigid ocean waters, but after all they'd been through, she didn't want to leave the tiger cat behind, either.

She unclipped the sonar detector from her belt. She had borrowed it from the *Roost*'s sensor array. "This says the sub should be right over here." They swam another hundred feet, strafing the ground with their headlamps.

Little bits of wreckage dotted the murky landscape. A door here, a wall panel there. They followed the trail until they found the *Cichlid*. The submarine had half-collapsed when it struck the ocean floor. Rubble spilled out in a circle around the sub.

Large patches of the hull had broken, forming holes. The sub looked like the carcass of a big whale that had died and been picked at by scavengers.

"This is it," Evie said, steeling herself against what lay ahead. Niels Bohr nuzzled against her arm, fearfully.

Sprout swam forward. His confidence made Evie feel safer. "Well, let's go, y'all! What are we waiting for?"

She followed Sprout toward the largest hole in the top of the submarine. They swam inside. The light from her headlamp did little to illuminate the cramped chambers. The narrow hallways were completely flooded with water. The floor slanted at a crooked angle, like they'd been transported into some kind of zero-gravity fun house. Evie took the lead, swimming the length of the submarine's main corridor, past the flooded laboratories.

Evie's respirator gargled noisily. She realized she had been holding her breath. She tried to remember to breathe normally and clicked on the comm. "Sprout, please talk to me."

"What's up, partner?"

"Nothing, I'm just . . ."

"There's nothing to be scared of, partner." His voice was reassuring. "Ain't nothing down in these parts but us and the fishies."

"Fishies, right." Evie swallowed hard.

They neared Doctor Grant's lab at the end of the corridor. The glass windows were shattered and the door was jammed open.

Niels Bohr hissed, glaring at the lab.

"Well, come on, kitty," Evie said, waving him on.

The cat hissed again.

Evie sighed. "Fine. Why don't you go hide somewhere safe? We'll find you before we head back to the surface."

Niels Bohr mewled and swam away from the laboratory.

Sprout and Evie went inside. It looked different flooded. Clipboards and other bits of trash floated in the water: an empty tuna fish can, a moldy bag of trash, test tubes, and a gel-screen tablet covered in sickly green algae. There was an enormous hole in the wall, a perfect circle that opened to the outside of the submarine. She remembered when that hole got made.

Evie swam over to Doctor Grant's computer terminal. With the bottom of her fist she rubbed some of the algae off the monitor. The screen was blank. She had to turn the computer on. Any data from their experiments on the Eden Compound would be on this system. Evie searched around for the power button and found it on the back of the terminal. She pushed the button a few times, but nothing happened.

It shouldn't have surprised her. Most computers couldn't handle a juice box being spilled on them, let alone the whole ocean. But then Evie got an idea. Sitting beside the computer keyboard was an external hard drive in an airtight waterproof enclosure. If Doctor Grant backed up his data, it would still be safe and accessible on the hard drive. She disconnected the drive and put it in her satchel.

"Hey, Evie, check this out."

Sprout had found the mixing vat where Evie and Rick had combined the ingredients to make the Eden Compound.

"Is there any left?" Evie asked, peering inside the large bell-shaped container.

Sprout shrugged. A stream of bubbles gurgled from his oxygen tank. "There might have been at some point, but any residue is gone now. Mixed in with the ocean water."

"Oh," Evie said, disappointed. "Well, I found this hard drive. There's not much else here. We should head back to the surface, see what we can learn from it."

Before Sprout could reply, something struck the side of the sub. Everything shook. The mixing vat wobbled on its narrow base.

"What was that?" Evie asked. She turned to Sprout, but

saw that his face was frozen in a frightened expression. She followed his terrified gaze to the circular hole in the wall of the sub.

A giant eye was staring at them through the hole.

The robotic eye blinked. Evie paddled backward, trying to put distance between herself and the hole. The eye darted away, revealing that it was attached to a giant pink robot shark.

Chompedo was back.

Vesuvia's favorite murderous machine had seen better days. Chompedo's other eye was smashed. Dents covered his hard hull. His chainsaw teeth were chipped, broken, and mangled. His left jaw joint was stretched out of place, so his mouth hung at a gruesome angle.

Evie figured that after they had rooted the eighth continent and Vesuvia had gone to work for Mastercorp, everyone had forgotten about Chompedo. He returned to his last issued programming: destroy the *Cichlid*, destroy the Lanes.

The shark gnashed his chainsaw teeth and swam through the hole in the wall. Sprout and Evie had seconds to act. Evie kicked off the floor and swam for the door. Sprout took cover behind the mixing vat just as Chompedo crashed into it. The vat snapped off at its base and toppled over, landing on Sprout.

"Sprout!" Evie screamed over the comm.

"Evie, I'm stuck. Help!" She could see him squirming under the mixing vat.

"Hey, ya big guppy!" Evie waved her arms at Chompedo, trying to look tough. "Over here! Bet you can't eat me."

Chompedo spun his bulky pink body around and swam toward her like a bullet. Evie paddled into the hall, looking for a place to hide.

Wham! Chompedo smashed into the wall, crunching the metal partition with the blunt tip of his nose. Evie swam up through the circular hatch in the ceiling. Below her, Chompedo wormed through the broken barrier.

Evie turned to the front of the submarine. The wall ahead had buckled under the weight of the sinking sub. It looked like two pieces of paper crumpled together. There was no way through.

The harsh whine of metal on metal drew Evie's attention downward, where Chompedo thrust his mangled teeth against the circular hatch. He sliced through the metal floor, widening the hole. In a panic, Evie swam to the rear of the ship. She found an open door and ducked inside.

Evie stared in shock at the room around her. Metal girders supported glass walls around a set of chambers. Above each was a valve capable of expelling fire and death. Evie remembered that all too well. She was back in the volcano engine room.

The glass walls were cracked and the girders mangled. Scrap metal was strewn about the charred floor. On the far side of the room, she could see the exit.

Behind her, Chompedo crashed into the door. One of his teeth poked the back of Evie's wetsuit. She pulled away, and the razor-sharp blade cut a long slit up through the fabric. A wash of icy water flooded the inside of Evie's suit. She gasped and swam through gaps in the walls of each chamber, making her way across.

She was through the second chamber when Chompedo broke the doorway apart. He thudded against the wall of the first chamber, splitting the glass like thin ice before propelling his body through it.

Evie entered the third chamber, where Doctor Grant had sacrificed himself to save Evie. Not a trace remained of their encounter here. The room was completely empty. Evie swam for the exit, but stopped short. Chompedo slammed against the wall of the second chamber, and it shattered after a single strike.

He was never going to relent, Evie realized. No matter how fast she swam, no matter how quickly she evaded him, Chompedo's predatory robot brain would make him chase her until he caught her. Then he would go after Sprout.

She had to end this, now.

But how? *Think, Evie. Think!* She looked around at the empty chamber, at the broken glass and crooked metal. The robot shark was too strong. What would Rick do?

Chompedo smashed into the wall of the third chamber. A series of cracks bloomed through the glass where Chompedo struck the enclosure.

Setting her jaw, Evie swam to the top of the chamber. She inspected the nozzle at the end of the release valve of the lava dispenser. It appeared to be working. The control panel next to the nozzle was dark. Evie pushed buttons on the panel frantically. The display screen brightened as the lights blinked on. The nozzle moved lazily like an eel.

Calibration . . . Increase velocity . . . Adjust angle fifteen degrees. Evie usually relied on Rick for this technology stuff, but she was alone. She had to rely on herself.

Chompedo broke through the wall and swam across the floor of the chamber. Evie knew she only had seconds. She pushed the button to fire the blast of thermal energy.

Charging . . . The screen blinked, the energy bar crept across the screen.

"No!" Evie wailed as Chompedo turned his head up toward her. She tucked her knees into her chest, so her dangling legs wouldn't look so scrumptious. He opened his great mouth.

The valve released, flooding the chamber with bright orange heat. The beam of hot magma struck Chompedo full in the face. Everything hissed as the water surrounding the molten rock boiled.

The blast coated Chompedo, smothering him in liquid fire. He crumpled as it coated his body, melting his metal shell. The shark shriveled under the heat and weight of the blast, disintegrating the chainsaw teeth. His face caved in and his interior flooded with magma. The shark sank to the floor and was still. The magma spilled over the wreckage, encasing the shark in a charred shell of hardened lava.

Trying to catch her breath, Evie swam down to the wreckage and inspected the molten rock. The water around

Chompedo was as warm as a piping hot bath. Evie sighed with relief. The shark was in pieces, totally destroyed.

Evie took a final glance around the volcano engine room before swimming back to the lab to find Sprout.

THE LINE FOR WORK ASSIGNMENTS WORMED THROUGH THE TUNNELS OF THE WINTERPOLE

cave system on the eighth continent. Diana could not see the front of the line, nor the back. She couldn't remember how long she had been waiting for her work assignment, but her stomach rumbled with hunger and she really had to pee.

Diana had established a program that passed out work assignments, saving Winterpole agents from waiting for hours in lines like this. But her mother had wiped the program, and now the whole contingent of agents at the outpost wasted hours every morning.

Diana refused to stand in line for another minute. She stepped out of line and hurried through the icy corridors to an elevator tube. Maybe if she could explain to her mother why her way worked better, with solid evidence to back up her point, the older Maple would recognize her error.

The doors of the elevator tube opened and Diana stepped out onto the launchpad. *Whoosh!* A boy with wings zipped overhead. He raised a silver slingshot and snapped a stone at Diana. She ducked and the rock hit her in the shoulder, leaving a welt and a sharp pain.

Across the launchpad, a trio of Winterpole agents fired their icetinguishers at a boy with a huge hermit crab shell on his back. The boy slammed his shell against the ground, shattering the ice that had coated his armor. He swung his shell at the nearest agent, sending him careening back into the others.

Diana spotted her mother across the launchpad, crouched behind a stack of shipping containers. She had removed her earpiece and was screaming into it. "Take forms 32-A and 14-B down to the labor office. Have them evaluate agents standing by with the usual questionnaire and ask the high scorers to fill out overtime request sheets for additional payment and work hours. Then send them up to the launchpad. We are under fire!"

"Mom! What's going on?" Diana slid across the icy launchpad and stopped next to her mother behind the containers.

"Mastercorp!" her mother said. "We're under attack."

"So send out an emergency order to get all the agents to the surface. We have to fight them off. There are dozens of agents standing around down in the compound not doing anything."

"That goes against our protocols, Diana! This is exactly why you're in so much trouble with Winterpole. Why can't you understand that rules must always be followed, with no exceptions?"

The roar of hover engines drew Diana's gaze to the sky. A humanoid robot, or android, floated a dozen feet over their heads. The bottom of the robot's feet glowed red as the hoverboots pulsed. The robot looked a lot like her former fellow junior agent Benjamin Nagg.

"Well, well, well, if it isn't my moronic old Winterpole colleagues. Ah, it's good to be back." The metal boy's voice sounded like a mix between Benjamin and an electric can opener. "I'll be taking control of the eighth continent now. 'Kay, thanks."

Diana pointed a finger at him. "You're not getting anything, Benjamin. So call off your freaky cyborg animal-people, or whatever they are."

"You mean Aniarmament?" Benjamin's red eye lights flashed brightly. "They're my Brat Brigade now, and they'll do whatever I tell them. Brat Brigade! Fall in!"

The three robotically enhanced kids quickly ended their fights and rushed over to Benjamin. They stood in a line beneath him, looking angry and dangerous enough to defeat every Winterpole agent, and then some.

"What do you want?" Mrs. Maple asked, sounding even more disapproving than usual.

"I don't want anything," Benjamin said, settling his metal boots on the ground with a loud *clang*. "I have everything I could ever want—because of this!" He presented a piece of cyberpaper to them. Diana read the familiar paper with disgust.

By every island and isthmus, by every archipelago,

whosoever holds this document shall possess full ownership of THE 8TH CONTINENT.

"The Ultimate Continent Ownership Form." Diana's mother scoffed. "How do we know it's real? You expect us to recognize your authority as the absolute ruler of the continent?"

The razor-sharp teeth in Benjamin's metal jaw curved into a wicked smile. "Let's go ask the Director. See what he thinks about my ownership of the continent."

Diana watched nervously as her mother shouted, "Do you have any idea how many permission slips you need to have a direct audience with the Director of Winterpole? Your digitized cashew of a brain could not even comprehend the number. Guards! Detain this law-breaking loon."

As two Winterpole agents approached Benjamin, he said, "I have all the permission I need right here. Gregory?"

The shortest of the Brat Brigade pushed a button on his belt and a hatch popped open in the enormous hermit crab shell on his back. A black metal nozzle poked out and pointed at the guards. A stream of flame burst from the nozzle. The guards' business suits caught fire. They screamed in terror and ran away, stopping several yards away to blast each other with their icetinguishers. When the blue mist cleared, the guards were encased in ice.

A shiver went up Diana's back. Shaken, Mrs. Maple led the group to the deepest levels of the compound, where the Director of Winterpole had been in seclusion since his arrival.

The room was wide and round and dark. Diana and

her mother led Benjamin and the Brat Brigade inside. At the center stood a dome, with tubes curling up from the dome to the walls and ceiling. A layer of mist covered the floor. At the center was a dome crowned with a thicket of metal tubes that curled up the walls to the ceiling. Through the tubes an enormous video screen was visible. A representation of the Director's face covered the vast monitor, a mosaic of code, text, and symbols that swirled with each facial expression.

The Director bellowed, "What is the meaning of this disturbance?"

Benjamin raised the Ultimate Continent Ownership Form. "As you can see, I possess your precious UCOF. As such, I am entitled to all the rights and benefits of the supreme ruler of the eighth continent, no additional permission slips required! You work for me, Mister Director."

Diana's mother stepped forward. "Director, please explain to this freak how foolish he has been, and grant me verbal permission to arrest him and his accomplices."

The room thundered with overcranked volume as the Director said, "Physical possession is all the Ultimate Continent Ownership Form requires. It is binding. Whosoever holds the form is the supreme ruler of the eighth continent, and all Winterpole agents must follow the supreme ruler's instructions to the letter, as stated in our company handbook. The Director has spoken. End of memo."

Diana looked at the vague, emotionless face on the screen. How could this be happening? Her mother dropped her arms to her sides. Diana had never seen her look so disheartened.

The Brat Brigade snickered and gave each other high fives. Benjamin stuck the Ultimate Continent Ownership Form back into the storage compartment in his leg, then turned to face Diana's mother. "Mrs. Maple. I order you to arrest yourself."

Shaking her head in disgust, Diana's mother approached a Winterpole guard and took his handcuffs, then clasped them around her own wrists.

Benjamin watched the spectacle with a sharp grin on his face. "Mrs. Maple, I order you to flap around and cluck like a chicken."

Mrs. Maple glared. "You're joking."

"DO I LOOK LIKE I'M JOKING?!" Benjamin's eyes flared bright red.

With a sigh, Mrs. Maple flapped her arms and walked in a circle. She looked like she was trying not to cry.

"Bok. Bok. Cluck. Bok."

"Oh, this is fantastic! This is too good!" Benjamin's jaw clacked when he spoke.

The Brat Brigade watched uncomfortably as Benjamin applauded the woman's humiliation.

"Stop it! Leave her alone!" Diana screamed.

Benjamin turned to her. "What's the matter, Diana? You know your mother detests you. Why do you sound so upset?"

"Shut up, Benjamin," Diana said.

"That's not true!" Mrs. Maple cried, still flapping her arms.

"Oh, but it is if I say it is. Tell her, Mrs. Maple." Benjamin grabbed her by the back of the neck. "Nod your head if you hate your daughter." He shook Mrs. Maple like a doll so she nodded her head. He gasped in mock surprise. "What a terrible thing to confess. So come on, Diana. What should I do with her?"

"Let her go!" Diana shouted.

With a heavily modulated sigh, Benjamin released his grip on Mrs. Maple's neck. She collapsed to the floor, gasping for air. He walked away, saying, "As usual, you're no fun at all, Diana."

"At least I'm not a robot," Diana snapped. Her words hung in the misty air, but only for a second.

Fast as a rocket, Benjamin was in her face, gnashing his bladed teeth inches from her nose. "Oh, but you are, Diana. You most certainly are a robot. Beep boop. Always following orders. First Vesuvia, then your mother, now the Lanes. That Rick Lane, he programmed you so well, didn't he? Just like one of his computers."

Diana stumbled back, speechless.

Benjamin snapped his metal fingers. "Buzz, Kitty, lock her up in a holding cell. Mrs. Maple, order any agents who might be loyal to your lame daughter to lock themselves up as well. Loyalists only, from this moment forward! Winterpole has a big mission ahead of them. Kill the Lane family." Metal clanged as he clapped his hands together. "Ooh hoo hoo. This is going to be fun."

11

RICK DUCKED UNDER A LOW-HANGING BRANCH. ALL THE TREES IN THE DENSE JUNGLE WERE blurring together, but Rick did not relent. He had a mission. He had to keep moving.

After several more minutes he came upon a large tree with a rock beside it. The rock was shaped like an old TV set. He dragged the rock across the ground, exposing the secret passage into the Winterpole complex that Diana had showed him months before. He let out a sigh of relief. Thank goodness the entrance was still here. Step one of his plan depended on him sneaking into the Winterpole compound.

His father's voice crackled over Rick's earpiece. "This is the *Condor*. We're in position. Waiting for your signal."

Then another voice followed. "Copy that, Daddy-o. This is Groovy Ruby. We are locked and ready to rock."

Rick tapped the earpiece. "You are good to go, Tristan. You too, Daddy-o. Er, um, I mean, Dad."

Dad let out a wild whoop and holler over the communicator as his silver bird-shaped hovership, the *Condor*, roared across the sky. Huge black speakers were strapped to the wings of the hovership. Propped on top of the vehicle was a round podium fitted with a keyboard, drum set, and microphone. Even from this great distance, Rick could make out Tristan Ruby's silvery spike of hair. He slammed the keys, banged the drums, and hooted like a flock of tone-deaf parakeets, pumping enough sound out of the speakers to shatter windows and make a librarian faint. The *Condor* swung a wide arc over Winterpole's launchpad. This was step two of their plan.

After a few moments of epic noise, a squad of Winterpole shuttles took to the air, led by a winged boy with a shaved head. The *Condor* drew them away from the Winterpole complex.

Perfect. Nodding in satisfaction, Rick ducked into the secret entrance. The diversion he planned with his parents and the rest of the Science Circle had worked, and now it was up to him to free the captive Winterpole agents and re-take the complex from Benjamin and his cohorts. If Diana hadn't sent Rick that secret message warning him of the takeover, he wasn't sure what they would have done.

A chill crept up Rick's spine as he navigated the cold, dark tunnels. Benjamin Nagg had survived the destruction of New Miami, but at great cost. Doused in Anti-Eden Compound, he had become something *between* a human and a machine. Rick had difficulty imagining it, though Diana's message had been unambiguous.

And freaky.

Twice Rick paused to allow patrols to pass through corridors so they wouldn't notice him. He felt sick when he thought how these same Winterpole agents had happily served Scifun only days earlier. Then there was the so-called Brat Brigade, the team of animal cyborg kids. Rick had seen some early clues to what Mastercorp was planning a year ago on the *Cichlid*, but he had no idea this would be the final result of Aniarmament. It made his head feel like the crusty glob at the bottom of a yogurt cup.

He found the detention block deep in the heart of the compound. An icy door set in an icy wall obstructed his way. At least Winterpole architecture was consistent.

Rick withdrew a cyber document from his satchel. He had heard of contracts having a rider, a fancy name for something added to a legal document. This paper he had drawn up had an overrider, something unique to cyberpaper that could overrule any Winterpole programming. He waved it in front of the door. An electrical charge shot from the document and zapped the door's security mechanism, overriding the lock. The door swung open and Rick went inside.

Rows of cells lined the hallway. Rick hurried, checking the dark confines of each room for his friend. He found Diana in a small room at the end, sitting on the floor with Mister Snow and several other agents.

"I'm here!" Rick whispered. "Is everyone all right?"

Diana rushed the bars of the cell, reached through them, and pulled Rick into a hug. *Dong!* Rick's head banged on the iron bars.

"Oh, Rick!" Diana exclaimed. "It's good to see you."

"Yeah, it's good to see you too," he said, rubbing his forehead.

"Good?" Mister Snow sneered. His knees creaked as he rose to his feet. "Good would be if I'd never agreed to work with you lunatic Lanes. I used to be Winterpole's finest agent. Now look at me. A prisoner and a disgrace."

His words put a sour taste in Rick's mouth. "A disgrace would be following the orders of Benjamin Nagg because of a stupid ownership form. Use your head, Mister Snow. Are you a leader? Or do you let the rules lead you?"

"Rules are important."

"Because the rules serve the people," Rick said. "Rules protect the people. If they stop doing that, then they're no good, and they must be changed."

"Let me *out* of here, Richard Lane!" Mister Snow banged his fist on the bars of the cell.

"Are you sure?" Rick held up his hands. "That would be against the rules."

"Grrrr . . ." Mister Snow paced the room angrily. The other agents hid their smiles.

Rick used his overrider on the cell door and it popped open.

"Now what?" Diana asked, straightening out her agent uniform.

Rick led the way out of the detention block. "We have to find your mother. She holds the power. All Benjamin has is the Ultimate Continent Ownership Form. If we can get your mom to nullify that form, we can regain control of Winterpole."

"But Rick—" Diana stopped short, looking worried. "My mom doesn't have the power to nullify the ownership form. Only the Director of Winterpole can do that."

"Right. Him." Rick took a deep breath. "Diana, there's something that has been on my mind. Have you ever seen the Director?"

"Of course," Diana said. "I saw him right before I sent my SOS message to you."

"I don't mean on one of his weird video screen things or isolation chambers. Have you ever seen *inside* that dome? Or inside his private office? Have you ever seen the Director . . . in the flesh?"

"What is this boy yammering about?" Mister Snow growled. "We are wasting valuable time discussing this nonsense."

Rick turned to face the older Winterpole agent. "When was the last time *you* saw the Director, Mister Snow?"

"I shouldn't even answer such a ridiculous question, but the last time I saw the Director's face was . . . Well, um . . . Actually—no, wait. I think it was . . ."

"Have you *ever* seen the Director?" Rick asked.

Mister Snow's face went as white as his name. "You know, now that I think about it, I don't believe I have."

"So what does that mean?" Diana looked spooked. "Is the Director of Winterpole . . . a ghost?"

"Well, ghosts aren't real," Rick said. "But maybe the

Director is a sophisticated AI, you know, artificial intelligence masking itself as human. Think about it, a computer program is designed for efficiency and rule making. Who better to lead Winterpole than a supercomputer?"

"Unbelievable," Mister Snow said.

"Mister Snow is right," Diana said, "Winterpole having technology that advanced is pretty unbelievable."

Rick shrugged. "It's a long-shot theory, but I have a gut feeling. Think about it. He's tapped in to all that computer technology, he runs a mechanical organization that follows an inflexible set of rules, just like a computer. What if, long ago, the computer that managed all of Winterpole's systems . . . took over?"

"And then the computer created a human disguise?" Diana asked.

"It's possible," Rick said. "If the Director is a supercomputer and not a real man, then your mom does have the power to nullify the form and stop Benjamin Nagg. And if there is one person who knows the truth—"

"Yeah," Diana swallowed hard. "I need to take you to my mother."

ON MANY OCCASIONS THE *ROOST* HAD FLOWN OVER A SEA, BUT THIS TIME THE SEA WAS AN endless stretch of coarse sand. The Sahara Desert had more sand in it than Evie found in her shoes after running on the beaches of Scifun, and that was saying something.

Sprout looked out the window and hollered. "Hoo-wee! Look at that desert. And not a crop in sight. Are you sure there's a farm out here, Evie?"

"That's what Doctor Grant's hard drive said."

Evie couldn't believe the treasure trove she had found on the salvaged hard drive. After rescuing Sprout from the attack of the giant mixing vat, they had returned to the surface to examine the drive on the *Roost*. On the way back, Evie couldn't resist teasing Sprout.

"Evie battles—and conquers—a killer robot shark, and the heroic Sprout, well, he was done in by a bowl."

"It was a *big* bowl, Evie," he said with a Sprout pout.

Niels Bohr meowed in amusement. When they returned to the *Roost*, Evie plugged in the drive. To her amazement, it powered on. The files on the drive didn't contain any information about the Eden Compound, but in a sub-sub-sub-directory, Evie found a text file that read "Farm Access Code 244" along with some coordinates. Using the *Roost*'s navigation system, Evie and Sprout had uncovered the location of this supposed farm: west of Cairo, in the Egyptian desert.

"But I don't see nothing nowhere," Sprout complained as the flying tree hovership crossed over the sand dunes.

"Keep looking," Evie said. "I'm sure we'll find—hey, what's that?"

She had spotted something shiny and silver on the horizon. Was it a mirage? She steered the *Roost* toward the reflective strip. As they neared the target, they found a vast flat area blanketed with huge solar panels, each the size of a house.

There was an open space in the center of the expanse for hovership landings, and beside that was an operations building.

Evie steered her old hovership in for a landing and powered down the engines. Niels Bohr padded across the control console, stepping on buttons and flicking levers. Alarms blared, lights turned on and off. Evie sighed. "Maybe it's better if you stay here and guard the *Roost*, Niels Bohr. Try not to destroy it."

"Mrrowl!" purred Niels Bohr.

Evie and Sprout emerged into the hot, powerful sunlight.

A man in big sunglasses approached them, wearing a

plaid shirt and dusty jeans. Niels Bohr bolted from the *Roost* and scampered across the ground, brushing against the man's legs and purring. The man scooped up the tiger cat and scratched him behind the ears. "Niels Bohr! It's good to see you again, old boy. What are you doing here? And . . . oh! Hello, children. I'm Doctor Mahmoun. Are you lost?"

"I hope not!" Evie said. "I'm Evie Lane. This is my friend Sprout Sanchez. We're trying to find a farm."

"A farm? Out here in the desert?" Doctor Mahmoun raised an eyebrow as he scratched under Niels Bohr's chin.

Evie said, "You know Niels Bohr, so you must also have known his owner, Doctor Grant. I know this sounds strange, but Doctor Grant was our friend and he left us clues about a farm located right here. I thought maybe we'd find a hydroponics farm, or a vegetable-cloning lab."

Doctor Mahmoun chuckled loudly, looking up at the sky and shaking his head. "Oh, that prankster. I suppose I can trust you since Niels here clearly approves of you. This is Doctor Grant's farm. Right here. A sun farm. We built it together."

Sprout took off his hat and fanned himself, looking perplexed. "But farms are for growing food! If you took a bite of the sun, it would burn the roof of your mouth but rightly."

Evie snorted. "No, you goose. Solar power! They're farming the sun's rays with these huge solar panels, out here in the desert where the sun is bright."

"Precisely!" Doctor Mahmoun said as Niels Bohr pawed his chest. "Doctor Grant pioneered the design of this sun farm. It took us years to build, but the clean energy it generates would boggle your young minds! We get to spread that power all over the world. I only regret that Doctor Grant did not live to see its completion."

Evie nodded sadly.

Sprout stepped in. "Doctor Grant's notes on this farm mentioned an access code. Do you know anything about that?"

"Access code?" Doctor Mahmoun thought for a moment. "Oh, of course! Doctor Grant kept a private lab in an empty temple near here. But since he left the project so many years ago, the lab has been locked tight. None of us could get in."

"But maybe we can." Evie looked between Sprout and Doctor Mahmoun.

Doctor Mahmoun provided them with directions, but as Evie and Sprout were about to leave, he cleared his throat.

"If it's all right, I would like to keep Niels Bohr here, with me."

"What? You want to . . . keep him?"

Doctor Mahmoun nodded. "We're old pals. Besides, my puppy, Werner Heisenberg, could use some company. Judging from this cat's poor whiskers, he's about had it with action and adventure. Maybe just some tuna fish and a head scratch for you now, eh, Niels?"

Niels Bohr meowed his approval.

"Oh . . ." Evie felt sad, even though Niels Bohr seemed happy. "I guess that's okay. If it's what he wants."

Evie and Sprout gave Niels Bohr one last pet goodbye before returning to the *Roost*. They headed south and soon came upon a pyramid that looked like it had been baked in the oven too long. This was not a pyramid like the famous world wonder pyramids in Cairo. This pyramid was made of blocky black bricks that looked like they might crumble into dust at any moment.

Evie landed the *Roost* on a nearby sand dune.

Sprout tightened his belt. His lariat and trusty machete hung off either hip. Evie smiled at him. "You look like you were born to explore a hidden temple."

"Really?" Sprout tipped back his cowboy hat and gave his lariat a practice flick. "Why do you say that?"

Outside, Evie and Sprout got a better look at the pyramid. Guarding the entrance were two brown statues that looked like muscular men but with the heads of eagles. And they were huge, like the giant battling robots in one of Rick's video games. The two kids ran across the sand to the entrance. There was an open doorway about ten feet across. There was a flight of stairs that descended into blackness.

"Well," Evie said, "let's go."

Sprout said, "Wait. Do you hear that?"

Evie listened for a sound on the wind. It was the whine of a hover engine. She craned her neck to look up at the sky and saw an angular black shape fly across the sun.

"What in the whole big orchard is *that*?" Sprout asked.

The shape swooped down, revealing a hovership crafted

to resemble a nasty black bat. It moved fast, hitting the ground with a puff of sand.

The glass roof of the bat's cockpit popped open. Evie's hands began to tremble as she saw Mister Dark emerge from the cockpit and Vesuvia hop out behind him. Mister Dark carried a large weapon in his hands that looked like some kind of grenade launcher. Vesuvia pinched a pink laser pistol awkwardly between her fingers.

"Ew, sand! Yucky, grainy sand!" Vesuvia growled. "It's getting inside my stylish pumps!"

Sprout called out to her. "Well, then you shouldn't have worn heels in the desert, ya pineapple-topped fence post!"

Evie hushed him. "Vesuvia, how did you find us?"

"Oh, Evie, sometimes you're as blind as that old scientist pal of yours." Vesuvia sighed. "My mother's robotic crows have been tracking you ever since you left the eighth continent. Mastercorp is just like Santa Claus. We see you when you're sleeping. We know when you're awake. And we are motivated by commercial interests."

Evie tightened her fists. "What are you doing here?"

"Shut up," Mister Dark commanded as he approached Evie and Sprout. Vesuvia followed, but she looked reluctant, as if there was something more bothering her than just the sand in her shoes.

"Stay back, Mister Mastercorp," Sprout ordered, drawing his machete and pointing it at the large man in the business suit.

Mister Dark glared at Sprout. "Drop the machete, or

you'll swallow those words *and* that sword." He looked bigger than Evie remembered him, as if he'd been hit with a blast of gamma radiation, or was midway through transforming into a werewolf, or maybe he'd been really good about drinking his milk lately.

Sprout lowered his weapon.

"Give us the formula for the Eden Compound, Evie." Vesuvia's eyes met Evie's with conviction.

"Why are you helping this weirdo?" Evie asked her, pointing at Mister Dark. "After all the terrible things Mastercorp has done to you."

"That's none of your business," Vesuvia said. "Just give him what he wants, and you can walk away. Please."

Please? Evie didn't think she had ever heard Vesuvia use the magic word before. "Your survival is unlikely," Mister Dark corrected. "But give us the formula and I will make your deaths slightly less painful."

"That's not necessary," Vesuvia said. "Evie, just tell him what he wants to know!"

Evie squinted at her old nemesis. Was Vesuvia actually trying to help her?

"We don't have the formula," Evie said. "We're trying to find it, same as you." She didn't like tipping her hand like this, but she needed to buy time so she could think of a way out of this mess.

Mister Dark raised the grenade launcher and aimed it at Evie and Sprout.

"Don't shoot them," Vesuvia said. "They have

information that will be useful to us. They can't tell us if they're dead."

"You have five seconds," Mister Dark said coldly.

"Evie . . ." Sprout backed up nervously.

"Vesuvia, tell him to stop." Evie shot the other girl a worried glance.

"Mister Dark, I know they have the information."

"Five," Mister Dark said.

"You have to let me interrogate them."

"Four."

"Sprout, run!" Evie shouted.

"Stop!" Mister Dark aimed the grenade launcher at Sprout and pulled the trigger.

"No, wait!" Vesuvia said, shoving Mister Dark. The grenade flew wide, detonating against the base of one of the eagle-headed statues. The shock wave was enough to knock Vesuvia and Mister Dark onto their backs.

Evie tackled Sprout. "Look out!" They tumbled down the stairs into the darkness. Landing hard at the bottom, Evie looked up in time to see the statue topple over, barricading the entrance of the temple.

Sprout's voice came to Evie in the darkness. "We're trapped," he said.

DIANA LED MISTER SNOW AND THE OTHER RESCUED WINTERPOLE AGENTS THROUGH THE

complex to Mister Snow's office, which Diana's mother had taken over. Rick stayed close by Diana's side. She was worried. Her mother would be furious when she saw they had escaped and that the Lane family was once again meddling in Winterpole business and breaking rules. Her mother would have a Vesuvia-grade meltdown when they got to the office.

Rick pulled a detention file from his satchel full of cyberpaper and prepared for a confrontation. As they opened the office door, Diana held her breath.

Inside, Mrs. Maple stood on top of her desk, on one foot. Her elbows were jutted out, while her left index finger was stuck in her ear and her right pinky was up her nose.

Diana hesitated. "Mom?" she asked at last, wondering if this was all a dream.

"Diana!" Mrs. Maple's face went bright red. "Don't look at me!"

"What are you doing up there?" Rick asked, moving

into the room with the others.

"I am following orders from the one holding the Ultimate Continent Ownership Form, of course."

"Oh, good grief," Rick said, adjusting his glasses. "Mrs. Maple, please. Can't you see that Benjamin's outrageous instructions go against the basic philosophy of Winterpole?"

Mrs. Maple wobbled on the desk but did not fall. Impressively, she still kept her finger in her nose. "What does a lawbreaker like you know about the philosophy of Winterpole, Mister Lane?"

"Mom," Diana pleaded, "you need to nullify the authority of the Ultimate Continent Ownership Form. Winterpole has lost control of the continent. Benjamin has used the UCOF to establish a dictatorship. You've had your finger up your nose for hours! Admit it, the UCOF backfired."

"No one has the ability to do that," Mrs. Maple said. "Except the Director."

"Take us to him!" Mister Snow shouted over Rick's shoulder.

"I am your superior officer!" Mrs. Maple snapped. "I don't take orders from you."

Diana pushed Mister Snow out of the office. "Mister Snow, please, you're not helping," she said.

Rick stepped forward. "Mrs. Maple, please, get off that desk. Help us. You have the power. Give us access to the Director. We'll set things right."

"The day I take orders from a Lane will be a sad day indeed," said Mrs. Maple.

"Mom, please!" Diana stepped forward. She couldn't take this anymore. She had to speak her mind, in a way that made her nervous but happy too. For the first time, she was telling her mother, to her face, how she really felt. "You've never trusted me to do the right thing on my own, just to follow the rules, no questions asked. Winterpole is overprotective of the world, and that's how you've always been with me. But when I was on my own I was fine! Just like the world will be fine without all of Winterpole's rules."

"But, Diana," her mother said, "I have to protect you. The rules are what keep you safe!"

"Not every rule. The rules aren't perfect. There are serious flaws. We're slow to react and even slower to adjust to changing times. But I've made efforts to make Winterpole the best that it can be. Haven't you been amazed by how efficiently we were running things on the eighth continent before you got here? How hardworking our agents are? That's because of the changes I've made. I compromise. I adapt. I adjust when things aren't working. That's the way to be a successful rule-making organization—to remember that we're making the rules to help the people."

Diana watched her mother's face relax. She lowered her hands and foot, then looked over at Diana, Rick, and the other agents.

"The rules must be followed," she said weakly.

"Then change the rules for the better," Diana urged. "And follow the new ones."

Mrs. Maple hopped off the desk, filled with new life. "You're right. Follow me. I'll take you to the Director."

"Mom . . ." Diana said. "I . . ."

"Not another word, Diana." Her mother was all business, as usual. "Move quickly."

Mrs. Maple led the group deep into the complex, back to the Director's private chamber. With a swipe of her keycard, she opened the door.

The hermit crab boy, Gregory, was waiting for them. He turned around and ran backward at them, shell-first.

Rick stepped forward. "I order you to stop!" He held out a sheet of cyberpaper—a halt order. Blue electricity crackled off the front of the page, but Gregory broke through the barrier. Rick barely dove out of the way.

A pocket-size icetinguisher dropped out of Mrs. Maple's sleeve and into her hand. She fired once at Gregory and a dome of ice splashed across his shell. He shook, breaking the ice into shards. That shell was super strong. Mrs. Maple fired again, aiming at his feet and anchoring him to the floor with ice.

"Restrain him!" she ordered. The Winterpole agents piled onto the bulky cyborg. He swung his body about, trying to break free, but the agents clung to Gregory's thick shell, looking quite comical in their suits.

Mrs. Maple fired several more blasts of ice at Gregory, and soon he was subdued, coated in ice and stuck to the ground. Some of the agents were frozen to him, and they complained loudly. Against Winterpole regulations, Mister

Snow moved about the mound of ice, trying to pry his agents free.

Diana ran to Rick and helped him up. Rick nudged his glasses back up his nose. They walked to the center of the room, where steam hissed out of the Director's isolation chamber.

Rick banged on the metal. "Hey! Mister Director. Open up! I know you're in there."

There was no reply. He banged harder. He kicked the metal container. Nothing.

Suddenly, the back wall illuminated with the massive pixelated face of the Winterpole leader. "Who dares disturb the meditation of the Director of Winterpole?"

"Show us your true face, Director!" Rick shook his fist at the screen. "Stop hiding inside that bubble. Get out here and face us."

The Director's computer-generated eyes narrowed. "Winterpole Law Number One, Section One: The Director of Winterpole gives the orders. Winterpole Law Number One, Section Two: The Director of Winterpole does not take orders."

"You can't open the bubble, can you?" Rick smirked. He looked like he had just beaten the last level of an impossible video game. "Because there's no one inside the bubble. Is there, Director? Admit what you really are."

The Director's face shook violently. "I am the Director of Winterpole!" he bellowed.

"Rick, use your overrider!" Diana called to him. She

circled the bubble and pulled on the access hatch, but it wouldn't budge. Her mother and the other agents crowded the isolation chamber. "Help me!"

Rick drew his overrider and flashed it at the access hatch.

"Stop that!" commanded the Director. "Do not open that hatch!"

Sparks flew. The hatch popped open, belching steam into the room. Diana fanned away the cloud and looked inside.

A tangle of wires covered a school-desk-sized circuit board, which obstructed any "access" into the isolation chamber at all. Several more circuit boards were stacked in a row. Diana couldn't believe it. Where was the Director? Was Rick right? Was the Director really a supercomputer?

A round monitor on the top circuit board flashed. An audio waveform swirled as the voice of the Director boomed. "Oh no! You have uncovered my secret at last. No one can thwart the omniscience and power of Winterpole's great intelligence. Step away, before I vanquish you all with my, um, artificial mind."

Diana exchanged a look with Rick. Something about the hokey way the Director was talking puzzled her. He didn't exactly sound like a supercomputer.

"How did *you* come into command of Winterpole?" she asked the circuit board, unsure where to direct her question.

"I have always commanded Winterpole. The elegant code that dictates my actions has evolved over the decades along with the organization. That is why Winterpole has advanced so efficiently."

"Something doesn't add up," Rick said.

"I know," Diana agreed. "Help me with this."

She reached into the isolation chamber and tore out the top circuit board. Sparks flew as the wires popped free. Rick grabbed the next one with her and they pried it off together.

"Stop that!" bellowed the image of the Director on the wall. "I order you to stop immediately. Unhand my circuits! I am an invincible computer program! Please believe me!"

Rick and Diana kept ripping out the circuitry inside the dome while the Winterpole agents cheered them on. Down deep in the dome, under the wires, Diana saw movement.

"Hey, look!" she cried, grabbing fistfuls of cables and snapping them free like she was plucking roots from the ground. They broke, exposing a cushioned chair at the bottom of the dome, surrounded by televisions, computer keyboards, and a microwave.

At the center of the clutter was a chubby old man in a dirty T-shirt that struggled to cover his oversized gut. He looked like one of those guys who doesn't get off the couch for an entire football season, or in the case of this guy, several seasons.

"Oh, blast it!" the man wailed in a voice that Diana imagined a slug might have.

"Mister Director?" she asked in disbelief.

"Don't look at me! I am the all-powerful Director of Winterpole!" He held up his arms to shield his pale face from the light.

"So he's not a robot?" Rick asked, sounding disappointed.

The Director looked up at Rick. "No, but if it weren't for you two, no one would have ever found out! My deception was perfect! The best way to protect myself from usurpers and other unsavories was to conceal my identity. I wondered: *what entity would make the most intimidating leader of a monolithic, global rule-making organization?* The answer, of course, was a powerful supercomputer. I had to *become* a computer, and so I began to think like a computer. I asked myself, 'How would a computer run Winterpole?' And the answer was that the computer would need to create an illusion—pretend that it was in fact a person, not an AI. And so I created the illusion of the Director, the person, as a charade of the computer."

Diana squeezed the bridge of her nose and winced. "So, you're a person, pretending to be a computer, pretending to be a person?"

"And you fell for it!" the Director said proudly. "The illusion was sustained for years. Anyone suspicious would have to dig so deep and get so many permissions they would never find the truth, and thus I was able to sustain my command over the organization."

A loud crash, like a thousand panes of glass shattering, drew their attention to the room's entrance. Gregory had broken free of the ice and scurried from the room.

The Director flailed his arms. "What's that? Who's there? This assemblage is obstructing the viewpoints of my multi-directional cameras!"

"Gregory is going to warn Benjamin!" Rick said. "Diana, we have to do something."

Diana nodded. "Mister Director." She leaned over the opening into the isolation chamber so she could lock arms with the man inside. "Come with us to the surface. We have to negate the Ultimate Continent Ownership Form. Benjamin Nagg has taken control of the continent. We need you to stop him."

"Oh no! I created the Ultimate Continent Ownership Form as a contingency plan. But now we need a contingency for our contingency."

"Benjamin taking control was never the plan," Rick said. "We have to stop him before he hurts more people."

"But I'm the Director of Winterpole! I can't break my own rules just because I feel like it!"

Rick exclaimed, "Look at all the rules you're allowing Benjamin to break because he has the Ultimate Continent Ownership Form! He has violated countless laws. That must supersede the UCOF."

The Director nodded. "You may have a point, Mister Lane. Stand back, everyone!"

The agents followed their boss's commands and backed away. So did Rick and Diana. The isolation chamber began to shudder. Cracks appeared in the sides of the dome and it blossomed open, folding apart like a great metal flower. Wheels appeared underneath the dome and it rose onto its movers. The Director sat atop the walker like it was a spidery scooter. He used a remote to pilot his mechanical platform toward the exit of the room. "Follow me, agents! Other folks! We shall go to the surface and deal with these do-badders."

Taking a deep breath, Diana and the rest of the group tailed the Director to the cargo elevator tube. This was a square shaft where Winterpole agents could load hoverships for storage and maintenance. It was big enough to fit their crew, which now included Diana, Rick, Diana's mother, Mister Snow, the formerly imprisoned Winterpole agents, and the Director of Winterpole on his rolling platform. Rick pushed the button for the surface and the platform rose. Above, Diana saw the square of morning sky widen.

When they reached the surface, Benjamin was waiting for them. Three platoons of Winterpole agents surrounded the elevator tube, each with an icetinguisher aimed at Diana's group.

At the sight of the Director, whose face so closely resembled the digitally rendered face they knew, the agents hesitated. Benjamin pushed through the circle, his thick metal arms knocking agents to the ground with each shove. The Brat Brigade stayed behind him. The girl with the cheetah legs, Kitty, was perched on Gregory's shell. Buzz looked ready to peck out the eyes of the first person who crossed him.

"And who is this superfan?" Benjamin asked in his cold, robotic voice.

"Oh, heyas!" the Director waved, wiggling his fingers at the crowd.

"Identify yourself," Benjamin snapped.

"I am the Director of Winterpole. You are a very naughty boy, Benjamin Nagg. A very naughty boy."

Benjamin made an iron fist. "I'll show you just how naughty I can be, Mister Director. I control Winterpole now. Why, I control the whole continent!"

"Wrong!" the Director cooed. "You're oh so very incorrect, Mister Nagg. As Director of Winterpole, I hereby declare the Ultimate Continent Ownership Form to be null and void. It doesn't mean anything!"

"What? No! You can't do that." Benjamin looked around, his red eyes flashing. The agents lowered their weapons, wondering if Benjamin's rule was truly over. The Brat Brigade backed away.

"Seize these continent seizers!" the Director ordered. The Winterpole agents charged Benjamin.

Buzz grabbed Gregory's shell and flapped his wings, taking to the air. "Run, everyone! Get out of here!"

Benjamin's hoverboots shot him skyward, and the others fled the scene. The Winterpole agents opened fire with their icetinguishers, but the Director's presence hadn't improved their aim.

Mister Snow barked orders. "Get after them! Man your hoverships, agents, let's go!" The agents leaped to action, rushing about the launchpad and climbing aboard their vehicles. A squad of hoverships took off and pursued the Brat Brigade south, over the jungle.

Diana turned to Rick. "I can't believe we did it. You saved me. And we saved Winterpole. Thank you."

Rick adjusted his glasses to hide his blushing. "Just returning the favor. You've saved me a bunch of times."

The Director wheeled close to Diana and Rick. "Now the question remains, what to do about you, Miss Maple."

"*Agent* Maple," Diana's mother corrected. She gave Diana a small smile.

"Oh, yes, of course!" The Director said. "I believe a commendation is in order, for your bravery, efficiency, and overall superlative Winterpole-esque behavior."

"A commendation?" Diana asked excitedly. "Me? Really? Rick deserves one too. We never could have saved Winterpole without him."

"I have something else planned for young Mister Lane." The Director cleared his throat. "I think you'll like this. You have proven yourself to be a defender of the world, well in line with the stated goals of Winterpole. As such, I hereby declare all past infractions committed by the Lane family, Lane Industries, and the city of Scifun null and void! Your records are clear! Penalties deleted!"

Rick gasped in surprise. Diana hugged him jubilantly as he grinned from ear to ear. Rick's communicator beeped. George Lane's voice crackled over the speaker. "Did I hear that right? My record's clear? Woohoo!"

The *Condor* zoomed overhead, corkscrewing in wild patterns. Tristan Ruby's speakers, strapped to the wings, pumped a triumphant fanfare.

"Dad!" Rick shouted into his communicator. "Have you been listening this whole time?"

"Of course!" George said over the comm. "I had to block out this maniac's music somehow."

"I heard that!" said the muffled voice of Tristan Ruby in the background.

Diana looked at Rick, shaking her head in disbelief. "I can't believe it. It's over."

"Uhhh . . ." George's voice crackled again. "I wouldn't count your endangered eagle eggs before they hatch. You kids better take a good long look at the sky west of here."

Squinting into the distance, Diana felt her heart sink. Looming among gray storm clouds was a massive black hovership, shaped like a deadly shark.

"Mastercorp," Rick said in dismay. "They're coming."

14

INSIDE THE PYRAMID, GRAINS OF SAND COVERED
THE STONE FLOOR, AND EVIE'S SHOES MADE LOUD
scraping noises with each step. She led the way down the
narrow corridor, aiming her flashlight into each dark nook
and cranny.

"Evie," Sprout whispered, staying close behind her, "Are
you sure we're going the right way?"

"What other way is there to go? We can't go back. I
didn't see any turns. The only way is forward."

The walls were lined with beautiful engraved hiero-
glyphs, pictograph symbols that the ancient Egyptians
used to communicate. Evie couldn't decipher the words, but
in some cases the images were easy enough to understand.
Farming is good. When you die, if your heart weighs more
than a feather, some lizard-leopard-hippo-looking thing
will eat you.

"Pyramids are amazing, aren't they?" Evie mused.

"Sure, I mean, they're mighty big and all, but . . . What
do you mean?"

"How do you move giant bricks like that, and build something *so huge*, thousands of years ago?"

"I dunno," Sprout said. "Hard work, I guess."

"Some people think aliens built the pyramids."

Sprout snorted. "I reckon Rick would give you a mighty lecture if he heard you say that, Evie."

"Oh, I'm sure he would make fun of me. But who cares? Sure, maybe aliens had nothing to do with building the pyramids. Maybe there aren't any aliens at all. But . . . I mean . . . don't you wonder? What's out there, beyond the stars?"

"I think the stars are amazing enough," Sprout said. "Especially the sun. We all live because of the sun. The sun makes the plants grow."

Evie felt a slight tremor in her voice as she spoke. "I want to know what's out there. I've explored all seven continents with my dad. I created an eighth continent and I explored that too. I've been to the bottom of the ocean. What's next?"

Evie pointed up.

Sprout stopped suddenly. "Hey now, look at this."

The corridor ended abruptly at a flat yellow door. Evie leaned her flashlight against the wall to take a closer look. A grid of squares covered the door, and each square had English letters on it.

"What the heck is this?" Sprout removed his hat and scratched his head.

Evie read down the left column of squares. "H . . . Li . . . Na . . . Oh, I get it! It's the Periodic Table of Elements."

"Oh yeah!" Sprout grinned. "Professor Doran taught me about this. It's the labeling system for chemical elements. I reckon it's organized by atomic number, right?"

"Right," Evie said. "2-Tor made us study it. The atomic number is the number of protons a given atom has. Each atom has a different number of protons. Top left—hydrogen. That one has a single proton."

"That's some mighty fine knowledge you got there, Evie."

She giggled. "See, I do listen! Now how do we get past this door? Any ideas?"

"Hmm . . ." Sprout scratched his chin. "What was that access code we found?"

"Two-four-four." Evie looked at the periodic table carved into the door. "Oh, I know!" She pushed the square that read *Pu.* "Two-four-four. The standard atomic weight of plutonium."

The *Pu* button slid back into the door, and then the portal swung open with a groan, revealing a dark laboratory beyond.

"Rick insisted I learn my atomic weights," Evie explained with a smile, snatching her flashlight back.

The laboratory was dark and empty. There were no lights, which made sense, considering Doctor Grant was blind. A standing sarcophagus emerged from the far wall. The coffin was shaped like a man, holding a crook in its hands, but it had the head of a cat—a tiger cat.

Evie laughed as she approached the sarcophagus. "You

always had a sense of humor, didn't you, Doctor Grant?" She pried the sarcophagus open, revealing a computer terminal inside.

She pushed the power button on the side of the terminal and it hummed to life. She did a file search for the formula of the Eden Compound. A window appeared, and inside was a round icon that said "Click Me."

Evie looked at Sprout, who shrugged. She turned back to the computer, determined, and clicked on the icon.

A strip of paper spilled from the side of the computer. Evie stared at the complex formula printed on the paper in black ink. She thought back, long ago, to the sub-sub-sub-basement in Lane mansion, where she and Rick had first learned about the Eden Compound that would change their lives forever. This formula looked familiar, almost like that same formula from the basement.

"This is it," Evie said. "I think we've found it, Sprout!"

Eagerly, she tore off the long strip of paper and stuck it into her pocket.

At the sound of paper tearing, sand began to spill from the keyboard and out of the cracks in the monitor. Evie backed away from the computer as more sand poured out. Sprout clung to her.

"What's happening?" he asked.

"I don't know!" she cried. "Run!"

The sand burst in a plume, exploding across the lab. As Evie turned, the computer broke open like an egg. A column of sand hit her full in the back, knocking her to the ground. She scrambled to her feet but the sand piled on top of her, weighing her down. She tried to push off the ground to propel her toward the exit. Sand coated the floor and swallowed her hands.

"Help—mrffph!" Evie cried, gobbling a mouthful of sand as she screamed. Blind, flailing, she pushed forward.

A wave of sand hoisted her up, and she surfed down the hall back toward the stairs. She covered her head so she wouldn't smack it against the stone ceiling. The wave subsided, dropping her onto the floor. She groaned in pain, clutching her elbow, which had received a good solid whack from the floor.

The stairs were in front of her. Evie scrambled up several steps and turned back, looking for her friend.

"Sprout!" she screamed over the roar of the cascading sand. "SPROUT!"

The boy's cowboy hat slid down a wave of sand and landed at Evie's feet. But the boy was not attached to it.

"Sprout!" Evie screamed again.

Then she saw him, swimming through the mountain of coarse grains, fighting to get to her. "Evie!" he wailed, his voice muffled by the noise. The sand swallowed him up to the neck. His hand reached out for Evie. She grabbed him and held his hand tight.

Another wave of sand crashed over Sprout, swallowing him into its granular embrace. His head sank under the surface and his hand tugged free of her grip.

"Sprout, no!" Evie cried. She flailed, trying to grab him,

but the sand swallowed his outstretched hand. Sprout was gone. The boy who had taught her so much about the fruit of the earth. About the beauty of the planet. About friendship and joy. Gone. All gone.

No. She had lost Doctor Grant, but she wouldn't lose another friend. The sand continued to rise, but she didn't care. She buried both her hands into the sand up to the shoulders. She swung her hands back and forth, searching for the boy that had given her so much.

Evie touched something. She grabbed on and pulled.

First fingers, then palm, then wrist appeared. An arm, and then Sprout, plucked from the ground like one of his vegetables. His mouth was clamped shut. His eyes were closed. His entire body was covered in sand.

"Sprout!" Evie screamed, trying to revive him.

As she slapped his face and shook his shoulders, another wave crashed over her, dousing her in sand. She hung onto Sprout so she wouldn't lose him, shutting her eyes tight against the sharp grains. She felt herself moving straight up, like a geyser.

And then, light. The sand pushed her from the peak of the brown pyramid like an erupting volcano, and the sand carried her down to the ground outside. Evie slammed into the sandy earth, feeling every bone groan under the strain. Miraculously, nothing broke. But the pain radiated through her. Sprout lay beside her, eyes still closed. She closed her eyes and clung to him in the hope that the earth would stop spinning.

A shadow fell over Evie. She opened her eyes to see a large man standing over her.

"Oh no," she groaned.

Mister Dark snapped his fingers, and then Vesuvia appeared. Evie thought she saw relief flicker across Vesuvia's face, but it was quickly replaced with her usual annoyed expression. Vesuvia rummaged through Evie's pockets and procured the long ribbon of paper.

"Is this it?" she asked.

Mister Dark snatched the paper from Vesuvia and examined it. "Yes. The Eden Compound. At long last." He snapped his fingers again and walked toward his bat-shaped hovership. "Hurry up, Vesuvia. Finish them off. We're going."

Vesuvia hesitated. Evie gave her the most hateful look she could muster, but she was surprised when Vesuvia didn't return the glare. Instead, Vesuvia bit her lip, displaying something that Evie didn't think she was capable of—regret.

"Vesuvia!" Mister Dark hissed.

The spell was broken. Vesuvia straightened up and aimed her hot-pink laser gun at Evie.

Evie was too weak to scramble out of the way. She closed her eyes. At least she and Sprout were together.

Pew! Pew!

Evie heard the sound of the laser gun firing and braced for the pain, but it never came. She slowly opened her eyes to see Vesuvia stalking off to the hovership with Mister Dark.

Vesuvia didn't kill them.

To the left of Evie's head, a small smoking crater had appeared in the sand. That must have been the laser blast. Vesuvia had missed on purpose!

Evie waited until the hovership took off and the coast was clear. With the last of her strength, Evie shoved her friend. "Hey . . . Sprout . . . Are you dead?"

Sprout groaned. "Yeah."

"You're dead? That's terrible news."

"Glad you think so."

Evie squeezed his arm, grateful they were both alive. But they didn't have a second to lose. The whole reason they were in Egypt—the Eden Compound formula—was rapidly on its way to Mastercorp.

"Come on, Sprout! We have to warn Rick and the others," Evie said, dragging her aching body upright. "To the *Roost*."

RICK SPRINTED ACROSS THE LAUNCHPAD AT THE WINTERPOLE OUTPOST. BLACK INSECTOID

hoverships, sent from the dreadnought, swarmed above him. Rick and the others had taken to calling the ships "bugs." The bugs pummeled the ground with little capsules, which broke on impact, spilling Anti-Eden Compound across the runway, transforming the icy ground into sheets of stay-fresh plastic wrap. He waved Winterpole agents out of the way.

"Move! Move!" Rick shouted. The Mastercorp bugs battered the top of the array as a familiar tree flew overhead. Rick ducked under the communications array for cover and pulled out his pocket tablet.

Rick called into his tablet. "Evie! What are you doing? It's too dangerous!"

"Thanks, bro!" Evie's voice was cheerful, as if nothing was out of the ordinary. "It's good to *be* back. Think you can make an opening for us?"

"Yeah, sure, no problem." Rick grimaced. This wasn't

going to be easy. He took off running across the launch-pad again, this time headed for the cargo elevator tube. He dodged all the nasty garbage the bugs were making on the ground and slid into the control console for the tube. He threw the lever, lowering the platform, while the Winterpole agents laid down suppressive ice on the bugs.

Down the elevator went, forming a long empty shaft up to the surface. Rick tugged on the lever as hard as he could, trying to make the elevator move faster.

When it settled to a stop at the base of the tube, Rick took cover in an alcove and watched the sky above.

With a roar the *Roost* appeared over the tube, swung upright, and dropped. The engines reengaged at the last second, buffeting the tree's fall. The shock wave knocked Rick's glasses clean off his head.

As Rick scrounged blindly for his glasses on the floor, Evie and Sprout emerged from the *Roost*.

"There's my favorite big bro!" Evie said, running to him.

"Hey, partner!" Sprout said.

Evie gave Rick a hug. "Where are Mom and Dad? Are they safe?"

Rick nodded. "They're fine. Come on, I'll take you to everyone."

He led his sister and Sprout through the twisting icy corridors of the Winterpole complex. Above them, he could hear the deafening rumble of the bugs pounding the sur-face with their Anti-Eden Compound capsules. After a few narrow escapes, Rick arrived at the entrance to the big conference room cleverly named "The Big Conference Room."

Inside, there was chaos. A hundred agents ran around the giant table in the center of the room, passing memos back and forth among the people seated. And what a group of people it was: Rick's parents George and Melinda, Mister Snow and Mrs. Maple, Diana seated between them, Tristan Ruby, Barry and Larry, and lording over everyone was the Director of Winterpole, whose face was barely visible over his globe-like belly.

As soon as Evie entered the room, Mr. and Mrs. Lane leaped to their feet and pushed through the crowd of agents. They scooped Evie into their arms and hugged her tightly.

"I'm so glad you're safe!" Mom said.

"I wasn't worried." Dad squeezed Evie's bicep. "Look at these muscles!"

Evie flexed and giggled. Sprout flexed too, showing off his veggie-powered vigor.

"You there, girl!" the Director called out to Evie. "Have you brought us the formula for the Eden Compound?"

With a frown, Evie said, "Mastercorp got it."

"Oh no! This is very terrible. What do we do?" The Director slapped his belly in frustration.

Mrs. Maple pounded her fist on the table. "That's it! Mastercorp is in direct violation of numerous Winterpole laws. Illegally invading the continent, attacking Winterpole facilities, theft of a dangerous chemical formula. The executive in charge of operations must be arrested at once."

"Let me issue the arrest order." All eyes turned to Diana, who had risen from her seat and raised her hand. "I will take down Viola Piffle and all of Mastercorp. I'll bring them to justice."

Diana's mother looked to the Director for help. "Diana, I know you want to help, but you don't have enough experience. I don't believe our fates and the fate of the eighth continent should be put in the hands of someone so young."

"You don't think I can do it?" Diana challenged. Rick was glad to see his friend standing up for herself, but he secretly wondered if Mrs. Maple was right.

Mister Snow rose to Diana's defense. "Agent Maple has displayed exceptional talent since her assignment here on the eighth continent. It is my expert opinion that she is capable of executing this mission, and according to Winterpole regulations, she is technically qualified."

"What say *you*, Richard Lane?" The Director wheeled his seat to the side so he could lock eyes with Rick. "You're friends with this girl. Do you think she can handle this mission?"

Rick hesitated. Diana stared at him, hopefully and expectantly.

Rick swallowed hard. He pushed back his glasses. At last he said, "I think Diana would do a great job."

Diana smiled.

"Done!" The Director wiggled in his seat, satisfied with his conclusion. "Agent Maple will lead the arrest team. Depart immediately. We haven't a moment to lose. The rest of us will remain here to plan a counterattack on this Anti-Eden onslaught."

"Yes, Director!" shouted all the agents in unison. Rick wondered how often they rehearsed responding to the Director's commands like that.

In the commotion that followed, as everyone rushed to set up for the next challenge, Diana approached Rick. She put her hands on his shoulders. "Thank you," she said seriously. "That really meant a lot to me."

"What do you mean?" asked Rick, slightly taken aback.

Diana said, "Well, you believe in me. You think I can do it. That means a lot."

Rick nodded. "Just be careful."

"I promise I will."

Rick wanted to say more to Diana, but no words felt right. She left the conference room, leading a team of agents.

16

FROM THE COCKPIT OF THE LEAD WINTERPOLE
HOVERSHIP, DIANA WATCHED THE MASTERCORP
dreadnought grow large in the view screen. She didn't like
the look of the enormous black shark, with its grotesque
underbite and lifeless white eyes, but even more discomfort-
ing was the lack of resistance her squad encountered as they
approached. Most of the bugs were on the east coast of the
continent, pestering Scifun and the Winterpole outpost, but
there were plenty of Mastercorp hoverships still fluttering
about. They weren't attacking Diana's ship, or the other
ships flying with her. It was almost like Mastercorp wanted
them to land on the dreadnought.

The jaws of the Mastercorp ship opened, allowing
Diana's vessel to enter without a challenge. Robotic claws
emerged from the walls of the dreadnought's docking bay,
pinching the sides of the Winterpole hovership, guiding it
to one of the catwalks and locking it in place. Diana had a
bad feeling about this. A hundred armed soldiers stood at
attention on the deck of the docking bay. At the front of the
group was Viola Piffle. Vesuvia was nowhere to be seen, and

thankfully, neither was Mister Dark.

Diana emerged from the shuttle with her fellow agents, each armed with a super-powered icetinguisher. She knew they needed to appear strong so that Mastercorp wouldn't brush them off.

"Mrs. Piffle," Diana said, trying to sound stern. "Your invasion of Scifun is illegal. The damage you have done to the eighth continent is illegal. You are under arrest. Please submit peacefully and come with me."

"No," Viola said quietly.

Diana's agents raised their weapons. "Do I look like I'm asking?"

"What you look like," Mrs. Piffle said, "is a foolish girl who has come unequipped to deal with the might of Mastercorp. Seize them!"

"What? No! You're the one under arrest." Diana's protests were ignored as the soldiers rushed the small group of Winterpole agents. Diana fired her icetinguisher, freezing several soldiers in place, but they kept coming, and soon Diana was on the floor. Her arms were handcuffed behind her back, and before she could call for help, a gag was fitted over her mouth.

As the soldiers hoisted Diana to her feet, she caught a glimpse of a small blond girl hiding behind a docked hovership. Vesuvia watched silently, looking frightened and unsure, not at all like the confident brat Diana remembered.

Before she could think more on the subject, the soldiers dragged Diana through a door and deep into the dreadnought.

**EVIE PACED NERVOUSLY AROUND THE CONFER-
ENCE ROOM IN THE WINTERPOLE COMPLEX. HER**
father had worked with Winterpole to set up a bunch of
surveillance monitors to keep tabs on the ongoing assault
on Scifun and Diana's mission.

Something was wrong. Diana was out of contact and
they couldn't get a read from any of the cameras on the
hoverships that had gone to the dreadnought to arrest Viola
Piffle. Evie and Rick had even tried to reach Diana on her
private communicator, but without luck.

"I'm worried," she told Rick and Sprout while the adults
studied the other monitors. "Diana should have checked in
by now. Maybe something bad has happened."

Rick bit the inside of his cheek. "Mastercorp must have
taken her. They're holding Diana and the other agents
captive."

Evie didn't want to admit it, but he was probably right.
Her time on the dreadnought had shown her that Mastercorp
would not go down easy. They would never turn their leader

over to Winterpole without a fight. She didn't want to think about what Diana was facing as a prisoner of Mastercorp.

"We have to rescue her," Rick said.

"Agreed." Evie nodded.

"I'm in," Sprout added. He was always so reliable.

Evie and Rick felt bad about sneaking off without telling their parents, but Mom and Dad would never let them go on a dangerous mission right into the heart of Mastercorp. They needed to protect their friend and to complete Diana's mission: stop Mastercorp and bring Viola Piffle to justice.

Evie, Sprout, and Rick went to where their beloved *Roost* was parked. The thought of taking on the dreadnought and a fleet of Mastercorp bugs with just the *Roost* made Evie feel like she was waiting in line for a roller coaster that had failed its safety inspection. Even so, she knew she couldn't back down. Diana needed their help.

As they opened the access gate to enter their flying tree, Evie heard a familiar squawk behind her. "Children, I say! Wait for me!"

2-Tor's metal joints squeaked as he waddled down the hall. He flapped his wings and clacked his beak. "I'm not going to let you rush off into danger unsupervised. This is outrageous! You spend a little time as governors of a new continent and everything goes up in feathers."

Evie wrinkled her nose. "2-Tor, what are you talking about?"

"You are still children! You need a responsible bird to look after you."

Rick laughed. "Well, come on then, 2-Tor. Let's go."

"Yes, Richard." 2-Tor bowed. "Although I can't say I missed these dangerous missions."

They climbed through the tree's catwalks, ladders, and corridors, reaching the bridge. 2-Tor settled into the co-pilot's chair and Rick took the helm.

Evie grinned, watching them power up the *Roost*'s subsystems. "If you ask me, 2-Tor only wanted to come along because Didi might be on the dreadnought."

"Ooooh!" Rick said. "Is that 2-Tor's pink robot-bird girlfriend?"

"How dare you!" 2-Tor crowed. "That is a sensitive, private matter."

"They were in love," Evie sighed.

"Didi and I formed a thoughtful and platonic bond," 2-Tor explained. "That's all."

"I don't think that's what Didi would say," Evie pressed.

2-Tor flapped a wing at her. "You are a mockingbird of the worst order, Evelyn Lane, I say!"

Rick flung the thrusters and the *Roost* rocketed up the elevator tube shaft and into the air. For the moment, Winterpole had beaten back the Mastercorp bugs and the skies were clear. The flying tree veered over the jungle to the west side of the continent, where the dreadnought hovered menacingly.

A series of loud beeps drew their attention to the front of the cockpit.

"Something's coming up on our scanners," Rick said,

flipping on the targeting computer. "Possible hostile objects."

"Where?" Evie ran to the port window and looked outside.

"Everywhere!" Rick said as a punk-looking kid with a buzz cut and steel wings landed on the *Roost*'s windshield. Rick had told Evie all about Buzz and the rest of Benjamin Nagg's Brat Brigade.

"Mrs. Piffle told us not to let you anywhere near the dreadnought!" Buzz said with a sneer. A six-inch metal spike emerged from his boot and he kicked the windshield, spiking a hole through it. Wind rushed through the cockpit.

"Look out!" Rick cried, flinging the flight stick hard to the right. The *Roost* spun on its vertical axis, spiraling through the air. Unrestrained, Evie did a backward somersault, crashing into the floor a second later. Buzz went careening off the windshield and out of sight.

Warning alarms beeped across the console. "I say!" 2-Tor squawked. "Are those incoming missiles?"

The vapor trails arcing through the air were unmistakable. Rick threw the *Roost* into a dive, trying to avoid the heat sensors on the missiles.

Boom! Blam! Evie clutched the back of 2-Tor's chair as she heard two missiles explode behind them. Then there was a deafening crash and the whole *Roost* shook.

"We're hit!" Rick said. "Damage report."

Sprout crawled to the damage readout display. "Looks like hover engine two is offline. Aw, drat."

"Double drat," Rick agreed. "Let's get out of this heat and then we'll find a place to land for repairs. Maybe on top of Mount Inspiration. It's not too far from—"

Boom! Another missile collided with the *Roost*. 2-Tor squawked in a loud panic.

Evie tried to control her breathing. The distant horizon rose and fell like they were on a violent sea.

"Hover engines one and two out now," Sprout said, reading from the damage readout display.

"Rick . . ." Evie grabbed his shoulder.

"Hold on." Rick tried to keep the *Roost* flying steady.

Something appeared in front of the *Roost*, like a silver bullet hovering in the sky.

"Rick!" Evie shouted. The bullet had blood-red eyes.

The gruesome mechanical face of Benjamin Nagg grew larger in the view screen as the *Roost* flew closer. Instead of flying out of the way of the hovership barreling toward him, Benjamin engaged his hoverboots and flew at the *Roost*.

"What is he doing?" Evie shouted.

"He's crazy!" Rick exclaimed.

Benjamin extended a fist and grinned wickedly.

"Look out!" Sprout screamed.

Benjamin crashed through the front windshield of the *Roost*, shattering the durable glass. He cut a slash straight through the large tree, splintering it in half. Evie, Sprout, and 2-Tor fell to the starboard side of the severed cockpit. Rick fell to the other. He struggled to unbuckle his safety restraints, but his half of the *Roost* tumbled away before he could get free.

Without control or propulsion, the split tree tumbled through the air. Evie held on to 2-Tor. The metal bird scooped her and Sprout into his lap and shielded them with his wings. Evie hung on to Sprout, wincing as the devastated remains of her hovership crashed through the jungle canopy and exploded on impact with the ground.

18

IN THE DEEPEST CAVERNS OF THE MASTERCORP DREADNOUGHT, VESUVIA'S MOTHER KEPT A private laboratory. Here she conducted experiments in biology and robotics, creating new attack bots like her ravens, or new steps forward in cyborg technology. Vesuvia hated the place. It was more like a haunted house than a science lab, but when her mother demanded her presence, she had no choice but to go.

Vesuvia was still shaking sand out of her shoes, making each step she took to the lab unpleasant. When she arrived, the doors opened for her automatically. She stepped into the dark, cavernous chamber.

The mangled skeletons of discarded robots hung from the walls like shackled prisoners that had been forgotten for a decade. Sparks burst from poorly insulated cables that ran in thick clumps across the ceiling.

A great vat of Anti-Eden Compound dominated the center of the room. Black metal catwalks surrounded the rim of the container, and dangling from a thick metal chain above the churning silver liquid was Vesuvia's ex-best friend, Diana Maple.

Diana's wrists were handcuffed to the chain. Her feet swung free below her. The sleeve of her Winterpole agent uniform had torn and the top button had ripped off. Her hair was a disheveled mess—an atrocious style, even for Diana—and she hung her head in defeat.

Vesuvia's mother stood on a black metal catwalk on the rim of the vat, studying a computer terminal. A mechanical raven perched on her shoulder turned its head and glared at Vesuvia with its red, robotic eyes. It clacked its beak and cawed at her. Vesuvia shivered.

"Come in, daughter." Her mother's voice was as cold as the raven's eyes. "You're just in time to interrogate the prisoner."

Raising her head, Diana looked fiercely between Vesuvia and her mother. "I'm not going to say one word. I don't care if you torture me."

"Torture you? *Tsk tsk.*" Viola shook her head. "I'm not going to torture you, Diana. I'm going to indoctrinate you. You're about to become Mastercorp's most important employee."

"I'll never work for you!" Diana shook a lock of hair out of her face. Vesuvia had never seen her friend speak so defiantly. It was impressive and kind of cool. She wanted to tell her it was good to see her. She missed Diana, but she knew if she said anything nice her mother would punish Diana more.

"Don't be so quick to refuse me," Viola cautioned. "I

have been improving the Aniarmament procedure. When I founded the program, my goal was to create the perfect hybrid of human, animal, and machine. I forged perfect bodies for them, and now I will forge their minds. New inductees to the program will be my slaves due to my invention, the personality override. Members will obey my commands, without exception."

Viola tapped a few buttons on the computer terminal and the floor began to rumble. Vesuvia fought to keep her balance. The vat of Anti-Eden Compound bubbled. Robotic arms reached down from the ceiling and clamped Diana from the sides in their steel grip.

Diana inhaled a deep shuddering breath. "Whatever you do to me, my friends won't let you destroy the eighth continent."

Vesuvia's mother burst out laughing. Her dark cackle echoed throughout the laboratory. Vesuvia wanted to cover her ears. Instead she crept over to a tool cabinet and cowered behind it. Whatever was about to happen to Diana, it wasn't going to be pretty.

"Destroy the continent?" Viola laughed even louder. "Destroying the eighth continent is the *last* thing I want to do. Oh, this is wonderful. After all this time, your idiot allies don't know the first thing about our plans. I'm not going to destroy the eighth continent. I'm going to destroy *the other seven continents*."

Diana's eyes widened. So did Vesuvia's. This was the first she had heard of this.

Viola's voice filled the room. "The Anti-Eden Compound devastates organic matter, and I have produced it on a massive scale. Once we wipe out every last inch of dirt and tuft of grass on the planet, the only livable place on earth will be the eighth continent. Billions of refugees will need a place to live, to settle and rebuild the human race. And Mastercorp will sell it to them. Millions of dollars a foot. We can name our price and people will have to pay it because we'll be the only game in town.

"But . . ." Diana said weakly, ". . . only rich people will be able to settle on your continent. The rest of the planet will die!"

Shaking her head in disappointment, Viola said, "Diana, we're Mastercorp. Why would we care about that?"

Vesuvia shivered. Her mother's words sounded so monstrous now, but Vesuvia had to admit she had thought the same way for so long.

"The time has come to urbanize the eighth continent. We need to mine the continent's unnatural resources. We need power plants, weapons factories, industrial and commercial zones. Once Mastercorp is finished, this will be a continent of asphalt and steel, the face of the whole planet, a sigil representing industry and money; and you, Diana, you are going to help us."

"Never," Diana spat.

Viola waved a finger at her. "Can I quote you on that?" She punched a big button on the computer terminal, and the robotic arms clamping Diana engaged. Bands of metal wrapped around her arms and legs, encasing her in reflective pink material.

"Stop! Let me go!" Diana pleaded.

"Do you like the pink, Vesuvia?" Viola gave her daughter a sidelong glance. "That was a nod to you."

The metal tightened, cocooning Diana as she struggled like a fly caught in a spiderweb.

"What are you doing to me?" Diana cried.

Viola turned up a dial on her terminal. "That discomfort you feel is the monofilament metal weaving through your cellular tissue. It will become excruciating in a moment."

Diana begged, "Stop!"

Vesuvia winced at her friend's pleas.

"Vesuvia, darling, why don't you come up here and help Mommy complete the procedure?"

"Vesuvia, help me!" Diana screamed.

Vesuvia turned away. She didn't want to see what was going to happen next.

"Vesuvia, don't make me ask you twice."

The light on Viola's bracelet flashed, and her ravens swooped down, snatched Vesuvia by the shoulders, and pulled her up to the catwalk, depositing her beside her mother. Over the vat of Anti-Eden Compound, Diana looked at Vesuvia with glassy, helpless eyes as tendrils of pink metal wrapped around her face.

Viola threw a lever, and the chain lowered Diana toward the bubbling vat. The girl whispered, "Help . . . Help me."

Vesuvia swallowed hard. She glanced at the computer terminal, then back to Diana. Viola wasn't looking. Vesuvia had a few seconds to act.

"Please," Diana said again.

Vesuvia's eyes flicked toward the computer terminal. If she could get to it before Viola noticed, maybe she could throw the switch and save Diana from dropping into the Anti-Eden Compound.

But before Vesuvia could inch any closer, Viola turned and wrapped her daughter in a hug. "I'm so proud of you, honey."

Vesuvia couldn't believe what she was hearing. After all she had done to try and impress Viola, her mother was finally proud of her?

Vesuvia closed her eyes and smiled. She couldn't remember the last time she had felt her mother's arms around her. All thoughts of reaching the circuit board faded away.

With a shriek, Diana plummeted into the Anti-Eden Compound, the silvery liquid surrounding her and soaking into her skin. The pink metal melted, coating her body with a hard metallic sheen.

Vesuvia looked up at her mother.

"What was it that finally made you proud of me?" Vesuvia asked. She tried not to think about what was happening in the vat below.

Her mother snorted and pushed Vesuvia away. "Oh, please, Vesuvia. You are a disappointment and an embarrassment. I will *always* be ashamed of you."

"Wha- . . . What?" Vesuvia stumbled back.

"I saw you eyeing my computer terminal," Viola said. "You think I'm going to let you ruin my plans, you little traitor? At least you're so easily manipulated."

Vesuvia bristled with shame and rage. "You used me! Get her out of there!" she screamed, reaching for the computer terminal.

Viola shoved Vesuvia and she sprawled across the catwalk. "You're too late. The procedure is almost complete."

Vesuvia watched helplessly as Diana's body turned completely metallic. Viola flipped the lever and the chain pulled Diana out of the tank. The metal bands had sunk into her body, leaving her body bulbous and unnaturally pink.

Diana's arms and legs separated into eight distinct appendages, with deep creases running the length of each limb. They continued to stretch and grow, her whole body expanding to hang over the edges of the tank. The chain broke under the weight. Diana's giant metal body crashed to the ground, flattening the tank beneath her. Glass shattered, metal splintered. The catwalk started to collapse.

Viola raised her hand and two of her ravens snatched her up, carrying her clear of the destruction. Vesuvia scrambled back, her plastic shoes splashing through the spilled Anti-Eden Compound as she ran to the far side of the laboratory.

Diana's head swelled into an enormous dome, threatening to break through the ceiling. Her tentacles flailed, swatting at Viola. Vesuvia saw her mother tap a button on her bracelet, and the flailing abruptly stopped. That must have been the personality override Viola had mentioned.

The transformation was complete. Diana was no longer a girl, or even human. She was a giant pink robotic octopus. And she was Viola's to command.

19

EVIE WAS SURROUNDED BY THE VASTNESS OF SPACE. TRILLIONS OF STARS LIT UP THE COSMOS with their fiery, captivating light. Spinning moons, speeding comets, swirling black holes, pulsing quasars, roiling nebulae—all moving like cogs in the greatest machine in history, the universe.

Flying past uncountable galaxies, Evie saw something ahead. It was Vesuvia, floating through space, lost. Evie rushed to her, but before her hand could reach the other girl, Vesuvia transformed. Her body stretched and her face hardened. Her clothes turned the color of the night sky. Evie recoiled. Vesuvia had become her mother Viola. The woman smiled, revealing a mouth of grotesque shark teeth. Her mouth opened wider and wider until it was a hideous black maw that overtook her whole form, transforming her into the Mastercorp dreadnought. The robo-shark lunged at Evie. She flew away, her heart racing.

She rocketed to the center of a solar system, where Diana floated, shining bright as the sun. Evie's friend reached out to her and tried to speak. But sound didn't travel in space. Her mouth formed the words *help me*.

Evie held out her hand to grab her friend.

A slithery pink tentacle wrapped around Evie's neck. It pulled her backward and down. Then she fell.

In the sky above her head, the *Roost* was suspended. In a flash, the hovership exploded into as many splinters as there were stars.

With a gasp, she woke up.

Sprout held her hand gently. "Evie. Evie! Look at me."

Evie opened her eyes. The sky above her head was dark with rain clouds. A cold wind had picked up. She was on her back in the dirt, surrounded by trees on all sides. 2-Tor still had his metal wings wrapped around her. A big dent had formed in his bird head, and his eyes were dim. It was coming back to her now. He'd saved their lives by shielding them from the brunt of the crash. But at what cost?

"2-Tor!" Evie cried, shaking him. He didn't move. She crawled out of his grip and shook him again. "2-Tor!"

"He'll be fine," Sprout assured her. "We just need to re-boot him. But we have to hurry. They'll be looking for us."

The Brat Brigade. Of course. Benjamin and his minions would be after them, to make sure they finished the job. Evie looked around. The shattered remains of the *Roost* were strewn across the jungle floor. There was nothing to salvage. Broken scrap metal and wooden splinters, half the smoldering carcass of her beloved *Roost*. Evie felt like her heart had dropped out of her chest.

"Where's Rick?" Evie asked worriedly.

"He ain't here," Sprout said. "Let's hope he's safe."

Evie flipped 2-Tor onto his back and opened his access panel. She reset his power switch and pushed.

With a hum and a roar the metal bird jolted awake. "I say! Is everyone all right?"

Evie exhaled a sigh of relief. "I don't think any of us are all right. But you're alive, and that's good."

"I am an artificial organism and not alive in the slightest. Evelyn Lane, I have taught you better!"

Evie smiled, but before she could reply she heard the sound of snapping twigs in the distance. Shadows moved among the trees.

"That's them," Sprout said. "We have to go."

Evie helped 2-Tor to his feet, and the trio retreated into the jungle. They found a large fallen tree and ducked behind it. This was as good a place as any to hide and plan their next move. Rick was missing. They had to find him. He'd know how to get out of this mess. They were stranded in the middle of the continent, surrounded by enemies.

"Hey, look at this!" called a raspy voice from the other side of the tree. Evie flung her body to the ground and looked under the tree trunk, back at the wreckage. The little boy with the hermit crab shell and the skinny buzzard were studying the area where Evie, Sprout, and 2-Tor had fallen.

"Look at this divot," Gregory said. "And these footprints. They were here."

Buzz nodded in agreement.

"Spread out. They can't have gotten far."

Evie swallowed hard. Their hiding place wasn't going to last for long.

WHY DID EVERYTHING FEEL . . . PURPLE?
RICK OPENED HIS EYES. THE WORLD HAD

turned upside down. The earth was above his head, and a forest of inverted trees spread outward.

Then he realized his error. He looked down, er . . . up, and saw that the pilot's chair of the *Roost* had become wedged between the branches of a jungle tree. Rick dangled helplessly in his restraints. Any sudden movement would dislodge the chair and send Rick to the ground far below.

Carefully, Rick reached out and grabbed one of the branches. Holding on tight, he used his other hand to un-clip the restraints. He popped free and dropped from the chair. Clinging desperately to the branch, Rick swung a hundred eighty degrees. The blood rushed out of his head, making him feel dizzier. The tree branch groaned and the chair broke free, falling to the earth with a loud crash.

Rick winced at the sound. He had to be careful. Benjamin would be looking for survivors of the crash. Silently, Rick hooked his leg over the branch and pulled himself up to a sitting position, where he had a decent vantage point of the jungle. Broken pieces of the *Roost*'s port side littered the ground. The wreckage would draw the attention of the Brat Brigade, but the dense thicket of trees would hopefully keep Rick concealed. Evie, Sprout, and 2-Tor were nowhere to be seen.

A soft sound on the branch beside Rick caught his attention. A leaf wiggled. Reaching out, Rick brushed the leaf to the side. A thin white worm inched across the green leaf. But it was no ordinary worm. Rick adjusted his glasses and studied the creature. It appeared to be made out of the paper wrapper of a drinking straw. Crumpled and bleach white, the only way he could tell the worm wasn't a piece of trash was that it had eyes, antennae, and a little mouth that was nibbling on the leaf.

Fascinating. Rick puzzled over the little creature. How was such a thing possible? Some side effect of the Eden Compound, or a mixture of it with the Anti-Eden Compound? The Eden Compound transformed garbage, inanimate and artificial materials, into dirt, water, and grass. Grass. Grass was a plant, a living thing. If it was possible to transform trash into a living plant, why not a living animal, too?

Cluf, cluf! The sound came from the branch to Rick's right. He turned and saw the most fantastic creature. Its head was bright white, shaped like a Styrofoam hamburger carton, and it stood on legs of empty rolls of bathroom tissue. It looked a little like a frog.

The creature snapped its "mouth." *Cluf, cluf!* It hopped to another branch, and then another, and then leaped to the next tree.

"Hey, wait!" Rick called out. He looked for some way to chase after the animal, but the branches weren't thick enough to support his weight. Then he spotted the vines tangled among the treetops. *Brilliant!* Professor Doran had genetically engineered these trees to have thick vines to swing on. He knew how much Evie and Sprout liked climbing trees.

Rick reached up and grabbed a heavy vine. He untangled the end of it and held on tight with both hands. He took a deep breath. If the Rick from a year ago could somehow time travel and see himself now, he wouldn't have believed his bespectacled eyes. Because now, Rick didn't worry that swinging from jungle vines was dangerous. He thought it was fun.

Leaping from his perch in the tree, Rick swung in a broad arc, pursuing the trash frog. At the far end of the swing, Rick grabbed another vine and held on. The vine tore free and his swing through the jungle continued. Wind whipped his hair. His heart beat excitedly in his chest. He felt so alive!

The vine snapped halfway through his swing.

"Waaaah!" Rick screamed as he fell to the jungle floor. He landed facedown on the spongy earth in a pile of dead leaves. He chuckled to himself. His hovership had been blown out of the sky. Against all odds he had survived the fall, only to immediately push his luck by swinging on vines. At least no one was around to see him fall.

He rose to his knees, and froze. A foot away was a pair of cheetah legs. Robotic cheetah legs. His gaze moved up the legs to where they attached to the body of a very human girl. Her wide brown eyes looked as surprised to see Rick as he was to see her.

"Oh, hi," Rick said and gave her a little wave.

**WHAT WOULD RICK DO? EVIE PONDERED THIS
QUESTION WHILE TRYING NOT TO BREATHE, OR**
move, or even think too loudly. Shell-boy and Punk Buzzard
were still after them, scouring the dense jungle for traces of
her, Sprout, and 2-Tor.

"We gotta take them varmints out," Sprout whispered.

"To dinner?" 2-Tor asked, sounding confused. "But they
want to kill us!"

"Shh!" Evie hissed. "Quiet. Let me think."

The footsteps of their enemies grew louder.

"We can make a run for it," Evie said.

Sprout shook his head. "They'll catch us."

"Do you hear that? Voices!" Gregory was onto them.

"I will create a diversion!" 2-Tor sat up straight.

"But how will you escape?" Evie asked.

"You forget," 2-Tor waved a few feathers at her. "I have
wings."

With a great crash, Gregory's enormous shell burst
through the fallen tree they had been hiding behind. Evie

and Sprout dove out of the way.

Buzz leaped onto Gregory's shoulder and laughed. "Haha! That's two trees we've smashed today, Gregory."

"I say, run, children!" 2-Tor flew straight into Gregory's face, blocking his vision with a flurry silver wings. Buzz screamed in surprise, falling off his companion and landing hard on his back.

"Run!" Evie shouted, grabbing Sprout by the hand and sprinting through the jungle.

Her mouth went dry. She was sprinting so fast she was running out of breath. She glanced behind her and saw Buzz flying low to the ground, glaring at Evie hatefully as he narrowed the distance between them.

"Try to lose him in the trees!" Sprout urged. They dashed between two large trees and then wove between more densely packed trunks.

Evie gulped for air. "Sprout, do you still have your lasso?"

"Yeah, why?" He unclipped the coil of rope from his belt.

"Give me one end. I have an idea."

He grinned. "Oh, I reckon I get what you're doing. Hoo-wee!" He tossed her one end of his lasso and picked up speed. They ran as fast as they could, gaining a few feet on Buzz, who flapped his shining wings to accelerate.

"Now!" Evie shouted. She stopped short, dropped to the left, and pulled the lasso tight. Sprout dove right and did the same.

"What, no!" Buzz raised his arms to shield his face as he slammed full speed into the rope, which had become an effective trip wire. He did a somersault and landed facedown in the dirt.

"Hoo-wee!" Sprout cheered. "Look at us using our noggins. I bet a billion broccoli Rick would be mighty proud of our smart thinking."

"Yeah," Evie gasped, trying to catch her breath. "I bet you're right."

"Oh dear me, please help! Look out!"

Evie turned to see Gregory barreling toward them. A hatch had opened in his shell and a robotic propeller with a chainsaw on either end spun above his head, slicing through trees on either side of him. 2-Tor clung to the boy's head with his wings, flapping like a caffeinated pennant.

Sprout gawked at the charging shell-armored body. "I say, this looks dreadful."

"Hoo-wee," Evie said. "I reckon y'all are right about that."

22

THE CHEETAH GIRL WAS AN INCH TALLER THAN RICK, WEARING A TRIM BLACK JUMPSUIT AND A high bun of dark hair. Her pants were rolled above her knees to show off the agile metal legs, which were decorated with cheetah spots. She bounced back at the sight of Rick and crouched close to the ground, placing her palms on the earth for balance. She glared at him, although Rick saw something else besides anger behind her eyes. It wasn't fear. No, it was compassion.

"Hi, I'm Rick," he said hesitantly.

"I know who you are," she said. "And I know I'm not supposed to listen to a word you say."

"Well, you work for Mastercorp under Benjamin Robot-Face, so excuse me if I don't think you're the best judge of character," Rick said.

"Mastercorp gave me more than you ever could."

"What do you mean?" Rick asked. He sat down and crossed his legs. For some reason, he felt like he could trust this girl and he knew that she wouldn't hurt him.

"My parents were marathon runners. They trained all the time and traveled the world, competing in races. I would go with them. As soon as I could walk, I ran. And then . . ." She reached down and touched her thigh where the prosthetic met her flesh. "After I lost my legs, I thought I would never run again. But Mastercorp offered me a place in their experimental program. They built these prostheses for me. Now I'm the fastest kid on earth."

She hopped up and down, demonstrating the springiness of her step with each jump. "We all have stories like that. Buzz and Gregory grew up as orphans. There were a bunch of others in the program too, but . . . they didn't survive the testing process."

Rick said, "Mastercorp's experiments killed them, you mean. I'm glad Mastercorp gave you back your legs, but you must see all the other wicked things that company has done."

The girl frowned. "When I was offered a place in Mastercorp's experimental cyborg program, my family left our home in Kenya and moved to New Miami so they could be close to me during the program. But then Mastercorp destroyed New Miami with Anti-Eden Compound, and my parents . . ." She looked away as a tear rolled down her cheek. "I know Mastercorp is evil, but now that my parents are gone, I have nowhere else to go."

"I'm sorry," Rick said, feeling his own eyes well up.

She nodded sadly.

"What's your name?" he asked.

"I'm Kitty," she said, wiping her eyes. "Sorry."

Rick wiped his eyes as well. "Don't apologize. I know how much it hurts to lose someone you care about."

They were quiet for a while, listening to the sounds of the jungle.

"Your legs are super cool," Rick said. "What do they feel like?"

Kitty shrugged, beginning to look and sound relaxed. "Oh, I don't know. Like standing on bicycle pedals, kinda. Each joint has a little cushion of air inside, which makes them move smoothly. Each one has a little computer in it too, which analyzes impact data, stride consistency, and other stuff to help me increase speed and improve balance."

"Fascinating," Rick said. If only his father could hear this! He thought his dad's work in robotics could contribute a lot to biomechatronic advances like Kitty and her friends.

"You know, you don't seem like a tyrannical monster," Kitty admitted.

Rick snorted. "Is that what Benjamin said? Oh boy. Listen to your gut. Just look at the way Benjamin treats you guys. He's the tyrannical monster. We're the good guys, Kitty."

Kitty sighed. "Maybe you're right."

A burst of static came from the communicator on Kitty's hip. Benjamin's voice emerged. "Kitty! Have you found that walking redheaded corpse yet?"

Kitty gasped and took off running through the jungle.

Rick scrambled to his feet. "Wait! Come back! I need your help to find my sister and my friends!"

Thanks to her cheetah legs, Kitty was so fast Rick knew he couldn't hope to catch up. But he *had* to talk to her. He felt like he had almost convinced Kitty to leave Mastercorp behind. If only he could talk to her for just another second. Rick ran as fast as he could, gasping for breath, until a dagger of pain filled his stomach and his legs burned, but still he kept running.

He could see Kitty up ahead, and so he put on a burst of speed, only to realize too late that Kitty had stopped running and was now standing still. Rick tried to skid to a stop but tumbled forward and landed in a heap in the middle of a clearing.

Kitty stared at Rick in surprise.

The mechanical face of Benjamin Nagg was less surprised and very far from amused.

23

"LOOK OUT!" EVIE SCREAMED AS CRAB BOY CHARGED. SHE SIDESTEPPED, POSITIONING HERSELF in front of a large tree.

Sprout grabbed the captive Buzz and dragged him out of the other boy's path. "Evie! What are you doing? He's going to hit you."

Gregory's chainsaws spun wildly. 2-Tor kept his head low and held on to the boy's shell as hard as he could.

Evie watched carefully as they got closer. Closer.

"Evie!" Sprout shouted. "You gotta git!"

"Not yet," she replied. She tensed, waiting. Waiting.

Gregory dove at Evie. 2-Tor couldn't hold on any longer and fell off. He hit the ground and rolled away.

At the last second, Evie jumped out of the way. Gregory smashed into the big tree at full speed, burying the chainsaws in the bark. The boy slumped and hung, dangling from the metal arm in his shell, unconscious.

"Hoo-wee! There you go again!" Sprout grinned as he used his lasso to tie Buzz's hands behind his back.

Evie grinned. She had used her brain and her speed to bring down an opponent much bigger than herself. Rick would be proud. "Thanks, Sprout."

Buzz struggled against the lasso. "What are you going to do with us?"

Evie looked over at him. "What do you mean *do* with you? All we wanted was for you to stop trying to kill us."

"Well, then I guess you should let us go," Buzz suggested.

"Nice try!" Evie grinned. "I think you should tell me where my brother is."

Buzz shrugged. "No clue."

"Then why don't you take us to your boss? I'm sure he has an idea."

Buzz glared at Evie for what felt like a million years, but finally agreed to lead the group through the jungle. They roused Gregory, extracted him from the tree, and they were on their way.

After a short walk through the dense jungle, they emerged into an open area the size of a decent campsite. Rick sat on the ground by a fire, tied to a wooden post. The cheetah girl, Kitty, and Benjamin stood nearby.

Buzz nodded to them. "Hey, boss, hey, Kitty, guess what, Gregory and I got captured by these losers."

Their mechanical leader shoved Kitty out of the way and stomped to the center of the clearing. Benjamin's scarlet eyes burned into Evie. "You," he growled. "Why are you still alive?"

Evie shrugged. "Because *you* are the one who's trying to kill me, and not someone—you know—competent."

He squeezed his clawed hand into a fist. "I will crush your bones to dust, Evie Lane."

"I say, that's not a sporting thing to say," 2-Tor commented.

"And you I'll use for scrap!" Benjamin snapped at him.

"Uh, Evie?" Sprout sounded worried. "Do you have a plan, or are you just going to taunt the murderous robot boy?"

"I'm not scared of this overgrown cheese grater," Evie said. "He's going to let my brother go and allow us to leave the jungle safely, and he's going to do it right now. And the next time we go after the dreadnought he won't intervene."

Benjamin snapped his metal jaw like a piranha. "Oh? And why would I do that?"

"I'll trade you for your two buddies here. Buzz and Gregory for Rick. Two for one. Seems like a fair trade to me."

Benjamin laughed. "Those two mean nothing to me. Kill them if you want to. I don't care."

"What?" Evie asked.

"What??" asked Buzz, his voice filled with hurt and surprise.

"I hate these freaks!" Benjamin said. "I'm just using them to take over the continent. You think I *like* them? You think I care if you kill a couple of them? Go ahead. Do it."

Evie hesitated.

"HA!" Benjamin laughed. "You Lanes are all cowardly

liars. Look. Here's how you do it." He kicked his foot and his hoverboots engaged. He launched himself at Evie, claws outstretched.

"No!" Rick shouted. "Kitty, please, do something!"

The girl with the cheetah legs leaped forward. In two large steps she passed Benjamin and grabbed him by the wrist. Then she stopped short and swung him in a different direction. The boots propelled Benjamin into the ground. He tumbled back to his feet and skidded to a stop.

"Traitor!" Benjamin snarled. "I'll kill you! I'll kill all of you."

Kitty dashed across the clearing and vaulted over the fire. Sparks licked her metal feet. With a sharp-clawed toe, she sliced through Rick's restraints and then helped the boy to his feet. This all happened in one-point-seven seconds.

Benjamin glared at his Brat Brigade. "Oh I see, so you're all turning against me?"

"Sprout," Evie said. "Untie him."

The boy obliged, releasing Buzz from his lasso. Buzz stepped forward, popping his knuckles. "You know, Benny boy, we don't really like when someone says it's okay for one of our own to die. So yeah, maybe we are gonna all turn against you."

"I'm down for some turning against him," Gregory smirked.

"You'll all regret this," Benjamin said.

A loud *THRUM* turned their attention to the sky. The Mastercorp dreadnought cruised overhead. Suspended below the massive black shark was a pink machine of tremendous size. It had a vast domed head and eight tentacles that stretched and twitched in every direction. The tentacles had suction cups the size of circus tents, and a series of hatches along each side.

"What in the eight continents is that?" Evie asked.

"I don't know . . ." Sprout stared at the pink robot octopus as it blocked out the sun. "But it's Mastercorp. And that means it's very bad."

24

THE BRIDGE OF THE DREADNOUGHT WAS LIKE A DEPARTMENT STORE ON THE BIGGEST SHOPPING day of the year. Mastercorp workers crashed into each other as they ran around the deck, issuing commands, filling out orders, and compiling data. The moment of truth was close.

Viola Piffle stood at the center of it all. Her mechanical ravens crowded the helm, perched on the command console, her shoulders, the guardrails, even the pilot's head. "Decrease altitude by two hundred meters. Tighten deployment clamps by three rotations. Charge the dispenser!"

Agents rushed to obey her commands. Vesuvia watched the chaos, for once not caring that she wasn't the center of attention. Normally, that would make her want to puke, but all this time with her mother had shaken the arrogance and bossiness out of her. She kept hearing Diana's anguished pleas. The only person who had ever been nice to her, and really meant it, had been in danger, and Vesuvia had not done anything to stop it. Now, all Vesuvia wanted was for Mastercorp to take control and complete their mission so this could all be over.

Tactical monitors hanging from the walls of the bridge displayed various spots around the continent: the Winterpole outpost, Scifun, even the dreadnought itself. She hated looking at the images of the dreadnought, with the enormous pink octopus—no, with Diana—spreading her tentacles across the continent. The guilt felt like a pallet of gold nail polish crushing her chest.

The image on all the monitors switched to a thick, ugly face. It was the head from the observation deck. The CEO of Mastercorp. "Viola Piffle," the head said. "Report in on a secure channel immediately."

Without a pause the images on the monitors returned to what they were showing before. Everyone on the bridge was quiet, like a ghost had walked through the room.

With a flash of her bracelet, Viola ordered her ravens to pick her up. As they carried her across the bridge, Viola snapped her fingers at Vesuvia. "Come, Vesuvia, let me show you how a professional follows orders."

One of the ravens painfully clamped down on Vesuvia's shoulder, tearing her expensive blouse. Vesuvia followed her mother into a communication room. The door sealed shut behind them.

The giant head emerged from the holo-projector on the far side of the room.

"Hello, sir." Viola said. "I hope you will see we are progressing on schedule."

"I want you to accelerate the plan," the head declared.

"By midnight tonight the Board of Directors wants the seven continents to be reduced to stone and ash. Your little eighth continent should be well into the conversion process."

"I assure you, sir, it will be done."

"And what of the Lanes?"

Viola stiffened. "They're not an issue. Mister Dark acquired the only complete copy of the Eden Compound. I have it now. The Lanes have no way to stop us."

"Do not disappoint us, Mrs. Piffle. You know what will happen if you fail."

"Yes, sir."

The head vanished. Viola shoved Vesuvia out of the way and stalked back to the bridge, where she screamed at the crew.

"Everyone who is crewing the octopus, go to your stations immediately. The rest of you, prepare to launch the North American assault. Mister Dark!"

The stern-faced Mastercorp agent approached. His tie loose and collar open, he guzzled a vial of his Anti-Eden Compound serum. His neck was gray and zombified, with bloated silvery lines where his veins should have been. Wiping his mouth, he said, "I'm here. My people are prepared to launch the attack."

"Good. You have command of the bridge." She turned to her daughter. "Vesuvia. You're coming with me to the command center inside the octopus. Your friend Diana is about to make all our dreams come true. I want you to see it firsthand."

Vesuvia could not think of anything she wanted to see less.

25

THUNDER BOOMED IN THE AIR. A RUSHING SOUND FOLLOWED, LIKE A TIDAL WAVE. THE RAIN CLOUDS had burst, and as Rick looked around the circle at Benjamin, the Brat Brigade, Evie, and the others, he knew things were about to get wet.

The rain dropped like a waterfall, splashing the ground all around them. The campfire sputtered out. The dirt became damp and turned to mud.

Above them, there was another strange sound, a tremendous groan that made Rick's heart seize up. The clamps on the bottom of the dreadnought that held the octopus in place released, and the enormous pink robot began to fall.

"RUN!" Rick screamed and took off across the muddy clearing, away from the plummeting octopus.

The others followed Rick's retreat, except Benjamin, who shouted, "That's right! You can run! But you'll never escape me!"

The octopus landed in the jungle a mile away, but the impact shook the earth. The closest tentacle undulated in the air before slapping the ground like a bullwhip. A wave of mud and rainwater surged over the treetops and knocked down the kids as they ran.

Rick tumbled to the ground. Mud splashed his glasses. In the hazy darkness, he felt himself spinning in a circle on his belly, sliding across the muddy ground.

Evie collided with him. He grabbed her and they slid together.

"Grab onto a tree!" she shouted.

"Good thinking!" Rick reached out and caught one of the larger trunks. He clung tightly to the tree. Evie wrapped her arms around his neck.

After a minute, the mudslide ended. The groggy, mud-caked kids struggled to their feet and looked around. 2-Tor was hunched over with his wing half-buried in the ground. Sprout struggled to pluck him free like a turnip.

"What happened?" Rick studied the scene.

"Is he all right?" Kitty asked, running over.

Sprout tipped back his hat. "Well, we were skidding away in that there flash flood, but 2-Tor got the idea to stake himself in the ground. Saved my life, I reckon."

"Yes, but now I am quite stuck," 2-Tor said.

Evie and Kitty helped Sprout pull 2-Tor's wing from the ground. Rick watched the sky. Another tentacle was swaying in the air, looking like it could fall at any second.

"You rotten scheming Lanes!"

Benjamin.

"Get me out of this hole so I can crush you all!"

The group followed the sound of Benjamin's voice. He was stuck at the bottom of a sinkhole not far away. He stood on a small rock fifteen feet down, surrounded on all sides by slippery muddy walls. His hoverboots were also covered in mud. He was trapped.

"Okay," Evie sighed. "Somebody give us a rope. We'll pull him out."

"Are you crazy?" Buzz asked, scratching his shaved head. "That guy tried to kill all of us. If we let him out, he'll try again."

"That's not how we do things," Rick answered. "We help people, even people like Benjamin."

Gregory sighed. "Fine, we'll help Benjamin. There's a grappling hook in my shell."

A roar of wind filled the air. The other tentacle fell through the sky and slammed into the ground. A shock wave of water shot up from the point of impact, which stretched for miles across the surface of the continent.

"No!" Rick shouted. "We only have a few seconds. We have to run."

"But what about Benjamin?" Evie asked.

"I will crush you in my robotic death grasp!" Benjamin shrieked from down in the hole.

"Forget it, Lanes," Gregory said. "You're on your own." He fled into the jungle to escape the impending mudslide. With a shrug, Buzz followed.

Kitty lingered, looking between her friends and Rick. She pounced over to Rick and Evie. "Okay, what do we do?"

"I reckon we run so we don't get hit by that!" Sprout said, pointing at the wave of mud that was coming toward them.

Evie turned to Rick. He understood her expression—it was a face reserved for moments of extreme crisis, when, no questions asked, he had to trust her. He nodded.

Crawling to the edge of the sinkhole, Evie said, "Benjamin! Grab my hand."

Rick held her in place so she wouldn't slip in. "And hurry up! We only have a few seconds."

"I laugh at your seconds!" Benjamin said. "And I shall poke your hand with my sharp claws. Poke! Poke!"

"Hey, y'all," Sprout said worriedly as the mudslide rolled closer. "We gotta mosey!"

"I say, we must speedily depart," 2-Tor agreed.

Benjamin gnashed his sharp metal jaw. "I will grind your bones to make my—" A surge of mud poured over the edge of the sinkhole, knocking Benjamin flat. The mud washed over him, burying him under its thick brown mass.

The mud knocked Rick's legs out from under him. He struggled to get up.

"It's too late for him. Let's go," Kitty said, throwing Rick over her shoulder. She sprinted away, her feet barely touching the mud.

As she ran, Rick looked behind them. 2-Tor flapped his wings, snatched Sprout and Evie with his talons, and took to the skies, escaping safely. The mud splashed through the clearing in waves, burying Benjamin under layers and layers of wet dirt. What a dull, unexciting way to go. Not at all the blaze of glory Benjamin would have wanted.

Kitty ran clear of the flood, leaping higher and higher with each bounding step. "Hold on," she instructed. They spotted Buzz flying up ahead.

Rick clung tightly as Kitty jumped, reached up her arms, and caught hold of Buzz's foot. He flapped higher into the air, above the trees. Just out of the reach of the mudslide, Gregory was escaping on foot.

"Man!" Buzz complained. "You guys are heavy."

The continent spread around them, with its wide carpet of jungle trees and three tall mountain peaks in the distance. The lightbulb-shaped head of the roboctopus formed a fourth mountain on their other side. The tentacles stretched for miles and miles, constricting the continent.

Squinting at the head of the octopus, Rick got an uneasy feeling. It didn't just look like a regular octopus. It had a face, one that looked uncomfortably familiar. It was something in the expression. Rick recognized the sadness in those eyes.

"Oh no," he moaned. "That's Diana. That octopus is Diana!"

2-Tor flew level with Buzz. Evie shook her head in disbelief. "How is that possible?"

"I don't know," Rick said. "But it's her. Look at her!"

Kitty frowned. "I think I know. Viola Piffle put her into Aniarmament. She fused her body with machinery and the Anti-Eden Compound, creating a new human-machine hybrid, just like each of us."

Rick made a fist. "We have to save her."

"What can we do?" Sprout asked.

Down on the surface, the hatches on the sides of the tentacles opened, and buildings rolled out. The octopus was full of prefabricated structures—houses, factories, military bases, and the like. The tentacles formed superhighways across the continent, covering the surface with Mastercorp buildings.

"What are they doing to our continent?" Evie asked.

"They're taking over," Buzz explained. "Mastercorp plans to urbanize the entire landmass and sell it off piece by piece to other corporations."

"We have to stop them," Evie said, determined.

Buzz gritted his teeth. "Yeah? I think they have the same idea about us."

A flock of black robo-birds emerged from a vent near the top of the octopus and flew toward the kids in the air. Evie shivered. "Those are Viola's ravens. They're bad news."

"Well, what do we do?" Kitty asked. "We're defenseless up here!"

"Hey, Rick! Evie!" The *Condor* zoomed out of the sky. Dad's voice boomed over the speakers still strapped to the wings of his hovership.

"Dad!" Rick and Evie cheered.

"Gimme one second," their father said.

He flew the *Condor* into the flock of ravens, scattering the robo-birds. Then he swooped around and hovered above the kids.

"Hop inside!" Dad called out. "I've been looking all over for you! We have places to be, and lots of stuff to talk about."

26

**THE *CONDOR* FLEW OVER THE EIGHTH CONTI-
NENT'S EASTERN SEABOARD AND LANDED ON THE**
Sudsy Bubbler, the capital ship of the Cleanaspot fleet. The
oil spill cleanup vessel had basically become a mobile headquarters for the cleaning company since the CEO, Evie's
mom, had moved to Scifun full time.

Dad landed his hovership in the *Sudsy Bubbler*'s docking
bay and led the crowd of kids, and one very muddy 2-Tor,
to the closest cleaning station. The Cleanaspot employees
were nearly giddy with excitement over the crowd of dirty
children, and they wasted no time hosing them down with
turbo-powered soap cannons.

The group then hurried to the briefing room, where a
strategy session was already in progress. Members of the
Science Circle, Professor Doran, Cleanaspot Executives, the
Director of Winterpole, Mrs. Maple, Mr. Snow, they were all
there—everyone except Diana.

"What's the latest? Get us up to speed." Dad slipped
into the seat at the conference table next to Mom. Everyone
standing in a circle behind the table leaned in close to listen.

Mister Snow spoke hastily. "We were hoping you could tell us the same thing. How did the scouting mission go? And what is your progress on re-creating the Eden Compound?"

Dad sighed. "Without the formula, I won't be able to re-create it. We can't undo any damage done by Mastercorp's Anti-Eden Compound. Preventing them from releasing their chemical bombs is the only chance we have of stopping them now. As for my little scouting expedition, I finally found these miscreants. So that's something."

He pointed at Evie, Rick, and the others. All eyes turned to them.

"Well?" Mom asked. "What did you see out there, kids?"

Evie hesitated. She wasn't sure how to describe the results of Mastercorp's latest twisted experiment. Fortunately for her, Rick spoke up. "Mastercorp is trying to turn the continent into one big city. They are burying the natural landscape under prefabricated buildings."

The Director of Winterpole flapped his arms. "What about the giant roboctopus we saw them drop from the dreadnought?"

Rick hung his head. "That octopus . . . It's Diana."

"What?" Mrs. Maple said. "Impossible! How dare you say that about my daughter?"

"It's true," Evie said. "Viola Piffle transformed her into that huge machine."

Mrs. Maple wailed, "We have to do something! I'll do anything to get her back. Anything! Please, Diana is all I have."

"Oh, so now you see how much she means to you?" Evie muttered, glaring at Mrs. Maple.

"How do we stop the octopus?" Mister Snow asked, sounding more concerned than Evie had ever heard him. "How do we reverse what Mastercorp is doing and save Diana Maple?"

Dad rubbed his chin. "Well, from the analysis I've done of the children in the Brat Brigade, I have developed a working theory. Kitty, you were transformed using Anti-Eden Compound, right?"

"Whoa, whoa, whoa. How did you know that?" Kitty waved her arms in the air. "We *just* met. When did you analyze us?"

"Uhh . . ." Dad scratched the side of his face thoughtfully. "On the flight back? Did you all forget? I'm kind of a super genius."

"So what's the plan, Dad?" Evie asked. She was eager to know how they were going to save Diana and the continent.

Letting out a sigh, Dad said, "The only way to save Diana is to re-create the Eden Compound so we can reverse the effects of what Viola did to her. And the only way to do that is to get the formula back so we can undo the damage Mastercorp has done to the continent, and return Diana to normal."

Rick adjusted his glasses. "I have the perfect plan. We'll launch an all-out assault on the roboctopus. Viola Piffle has got to be in the command center. We take her out and retrieve the Eden Compound formula."

Evie frowned. Viola was sure to be guarded closely

by Mastercorp soldiers, her mechanical ravens, and even Vesuvia. But that thought gave Evie an idea.

"I think we can convince Vesuvia to help us," Evie said slowly.

"Surely you are joking. That girl is a maniac. She can't be trusted," Mrs. Maple said.

Evie shook her head. "When I was with her in New Miami, and on the dreadnought, she seemed different. Not like the crazy bully I knew in school. The way her mother treated her was"—she shivered—"Well, it was dreadful. I think if I can just talk to her, we can get her on our side, to save the continent and stop Mastercorp."

Evie looked around the room, every single face had the same confused expression—like a mutant goat monster had asked them a trigonometry question.

"Sprout," Evie turned to her friend. "You were there in Egypt. You saw her spare our lives. Don't you think she has changed?"

The boy wiped his brow. "Well, shucks, Evie. I reckon she did, but just because she didn't kill us doesn't mean she's going to help us."

"None of you believe me." Evie pressed a palm against her forehead. Her head felt like a locomotive was chugging through her skull. "Because of what I did to the settlement. Because I helped Mastercorp. You don't trust me."

"That's not true." Mom stood from her seat and hugged Evie. "We're your family. We've forgiven you. It's Vesuvia that we don't trust."

"But she's changed. If you don't think people can change, then what do you really think about me?" Evie asked.

"Mom's right," Rick said. "Evie . . . the only Lane who hasn't forgiven you is you. We love you. But right now, we have to focus on the tactical plan for our assault on Mastercorp. We can't risk relying on Vesuvia."

Evie sank down into her chair, her head spinning. The rest of the meeting proceeded quickly as they planned the attack, assigning duties to Winterpole's agents, Cleanaspot employees, and the citizens of Scifun. A thousand hover-ships would be in the air—perhaps the largest such battle in history.

Evie spent the rest of the meeting brooding in silence, wondering if she would ever feel at home on this planet again. *Some mistakes are just too big,* she thought. Her loved ones forgave, but they would never forget.

Later, on the upper deck of the *Sudsy Bubbler*, mechanics made final adjustments to the tightly packed rows of hoverships. Pilots rushed to their vehicles. Long lines of Winterpole agents piled into hover-buses for quick transport back to the Winterpole complex, where they would get their ships and join in the fight.

Sprout and Rick walked ahead of Evie, talking excitedly about their plans for the battle, like it was some video game. Evie didn't feel that way at all.

"Koo ka-koo ka-KOO!!!"

Hearing her family's old bird cry surprised her. She turned to see Mom and Dad standing there.

Evie froze like she'd been caught with her hand in the cookie jar. "What . . . what did I do?"

Her parents smiled and hugged her warmly. Dad said, "We love you, Evie. We don't want you to fly off and forget it."

"And we're proud of the young woman you are becoming," Mom added, running her fingers through Evie's messy hair. "Even if we'd rather you stay home and do your homework than go off on adventures."

Evie returned their hugs gratefully. This felt nice, like home.

An alarm blared across the deck, breaking the moment. A Cleanaspot technician ran past. "Mrs. Lane! We're detecting movement to the south."

They ran to the edge of the ship and peered into the distance, toward Scifun. The dreadnought had come out of nowhere. It was charging toward their beloved city at full speed. And they were too far away to stop it. There was nothing any of them could do.

Holding her breath, Evie waited for the inevitable.

The dreadnought flew over Scifun, past the tree-scrapers, without firing a shot. Instead, it went out to sea, moving quickly to the northeast.

"Where are they going?" Mom asked.

Evie said, "If they continue in that direction, they'll arrive in North America."

27

**RICK AND SPROUT WATCHED AS THE DREAD-
NOUGHT FLEW OVER SCIFUN AND HEADED**
northeast toward the United States.

"It all makes sense," Rick said. "It's worse than we
thought. They never wanted to destroy the eighth continent.
It's the other continents they're going to destroy with the
Anti-Eden Compound. They're going to wipe out every hab-
itable place on the planet, except here, and then cash out
when they sell the land."

"That's a real pickle in our orange juice," Sprout said.

"We have to stop them, but . . . the mission."

"I'll go," Sprout volunteered. "Gimme a small posse
of able-bodied folk who eat their vegetables, and I'll bring
down that robo-shark and hogtie it before nightfall."

"But you're my copilot," Rick said. "I need you to help
fly my hovership."

Evie, Mom, and Dad ran over, as did Mister Snow.

"What are we going to do about that?" Mister Snow
asked, pointing at the dreadnought in the distance.

"I'll be your copilot, Rick." Evie smiled, looking at peace for the first time in a long while. "We made this continent. Let's save it, together."

"Okay," Rick said. "Evie's with me. Sprout will lead the mission to intercept the dreadnought. Mister Snow, can we trust you to field a team and complete the mission?"

"By all means, yes," Mister Snow said. "I will hand-select the agents to join us on the mission to stop the dreadnought."

They hurried to complete their pre-mission procedures, setting everything up for the big moment. Professor Doran had armed the carrying carrots with corncob rocket launchers and was doing a last-minute check on the walking vegetables. Mister Snow had wrangled two dozen agents to join him and Sprout on their mission to take down the dreadnought. Tristan had armed his most devout partygoers, and they were ready for a fight. Everyone who had come to the eighth continent, the continent he and Evie had created, was here, and they were ready to fight to protect their home.

Rick climbed aboard the small hovership he had picked out, a four-seat flying water cannon that Cleanaspot used for their toughest washing jobs. Evie got into the copilot's seat beside him.

"Ready to go?" she asked.

"Ready." Rick nodded, feeling nervous, but sure of their plan. They were going to attack Mastercorp head on.

"I say, children, wait for me!" 2-Tor waddled across the

deck. "You can't go into battle without adult supervision! Or bird supervision, as the case may be."

"Hop in, 2-Tor." Evie grabbed his wing and helped him climb into the backseat of the hovership. "It'll be just like old times."

The ship rumbled as the engine fired and they rose into the air. Rick squeezed the controls carefully. It wasn't the same as flying the *Roost*. He missed his old tree. They had lost so much. Doctor Grant, the *Roost*, maybe even Diana. Rick tightened his grip on the controls. No, not Diana. He was determined to save his friend, even if he died in the process.

"Hey," Evie clapped him on the shoulder. "It's okay. Just like old times."

Rick nodded and relaxed. "Right."

Sprout's voice came over the ship's comm. "So long, partners! Mister Snow and I are taking off. See y'all on the other side." Sprout's squadron rose from the deck of the *Sudsy Bubbler* and headed northeast after the dreadnought.

Dad's voice came next over the comm. "Now remember, kids, we need that formula. It's the only way we'll be able to turn Diana back and stop Mastercorp."

"But be careful!" Mom chimed in.

"I'll be ready to produce a batch of compound as soon as you get the formula," Dad added. "So hurry!"

"Copy," Rick said. "All hoverships, form on me. Launch!"

The fleet of hoverships took to the air, following Rick across the water, back to the eighth continent. On the way, another massive air force, this one of Winterpole hover-ships, joined the aerial caravan.

"Winterpole has arrived," Mrs. Maple said over the comm. "Our statutes indicate that it's time to kick Mastercorp's butt!"

Rick and Evie cheered loudly.

They flew across the continent, toward the impos-ing head of the roboctopus in the distance. The tentacles had flattened trees and split the land. The ugly, repetitive buildings Mastercorp had placed across the continent were eyesores, and already mines had been established to chew up the earth for its natural resources.

"Stand by . . ." Rick said over the comm. "Prepare to engage. Hold steady."

The vents on the sides of the roboctopus's head opened. Mastercorp's bug-shaped hoverships stormed out like bees from a kicked hive.

"Break and engage!" Rick shouted, flinging his own ship to the side, dodging a barrage of needles from the can-nons on the front of the lead bug.

2-Tor's head struck the ceiling as the ship spun. "I say, Richard, can't you fight a little . . . gentler?"

The rest of the fleet split off, choosing targets and fight-ing Mastercorp's massive air defense. They didn't care how many hoverships they sacrificed if it meant keeping the Lanes away from Viola Piffle and the Eden Compound formula.

Evie aimed the water cannon expertly, hosing the windshields of enemy hoverships, blinding the pilots. A well-placed blast on a hover engine shorted out its propulsor, forcing the pilots of the bugs to eject.

"Come on," Evie said. "We have to get closer to the command center at the top of the head."

They flew across the top of the roboctopus. From here, they could see Diana's face, which had a look of anguish.

"She's in pain," Evie said sadly. Rick gritted his teeth.

Above Diana's eyes was a strip of transparent material that indicated the main viewport for the command center. Rick flew past, trying to get a clear shot, but as he approached, defensive lasers engaged, zapping at their tiny hovership.

"Look out!" Evie cried.

He swerved to dodge the attack, and pulled the ship to a higher altitude. "It's too hard. We can't get to her."

The battle raged. Hoverships traded shots. The bugs took down a number of Cleanaspot and Winterpole ships. Scifun's contingent suffered the heaviest losses. This wasn't like a video game. Every fallen hovership filled Rick with pain.

Evie took a deep breath, like it was now or never. She opened the cockpit door. A rush of wind filled the cockpit, blasting the kids with air. 2-Tor squawked in surprise.

Rick screamed, "Evie! What are you doing? You're going to get us killed!"

She calmly unfastened her safety restraints. "I'm sorry, Rick, but I'm right. I can get to Vesuvia. She will help us. The only way we can get to the formula is from the inside."

"Stop! Don't! We'll find another way."

Ignoring him, Evie screamed, "2-Tor, you gotta fly!"

"My word," squawked the birdbot. "What do you mean?"

"Fly, you bird. Fly!" Evie grabbed 2-Tor by the wing and pulled him out of the hovership door. Rick reached out for them, but it was too late. They plummeted through the open air. Evie hugged 2-Tor's metal body and pointed at one of the open vents on the side of the octopus's head. Rick watched in awed disbelief as 2-Tor and Evie flew *inside* the vent and disappeared.

At last, Rick understood. It was all up to Evie now. All he could do was lead his fleet and keep Mastercorp's forces occupied.

SPROUT RUBBED HIS ARMS, TRYING TO WARM THEM UP. IT WAS FREEZING ON THE WINTERPOLE hovership. But when he tried to turn up the thermostat, Mister Snow swatted his hand like it was a fly.

"You may be in charge of this operation, Mister Sanchez, but I am still flying this hovership and it is *my* hovership and I am a senior agent of Winterpole!"

"All right!" Sprout held up his hands in surrender. "If y'all want freezer burn on your pumpkins that's just fine by me."

The dreadnought grew large in the front viewport. They flew in from above, so they had a good attack angle on the top of the robo-shark. In front of the dorsal fin was an observation deck, and standing on that deck was a tall, nondescript man in a business suit. Sprout remembered him from Egypt.

"There's that rascal Mister Dark," Sprout pointed.

Before the squadron could move in to strike, a swarm of Mastercorp bugs burst from the dreadnought's mouth and moved in to attack.

"Evasive action!" Mister Snow slammed on the controls and the hovership went into a dive.

"Whoa! Easy there!" Sprout held on to the seat cushion. The hovership pulled out of its dive inches from the top of the dreadnought. It flew along the top of the hull.

"Go! Engage!" Mister Snow shouted. "We will disable their defenses."

"Right!" Sprout said. He ran to the back of the ship and jumped out of the exit door. He dropped into a roll and tumbled across the observation deck. Sitting up, he saw Mister Dark on the far side of the platform, staring at him. His sleeves were rolled up, and he flexed his metal musculature. His arms looked nearly as metallic as Benjamin Nagg's.

"You?" Mister Dark asked, sounding disappointed as he chugged a bottle of silver serum. The veins on either side of his throat inflated. He wiped his mouth. "Not even a Lane? Not even their stupid robot bird? They sent *you* to deal with me?"

Sprout pointed a finger at Mister Dark. "You're an unnatural rascal. I'm gonna take you down."

"How?" Mister Dark sneered and flexed. "I have the strength of a hundred men. My skin can stop bullets."

"I'll do it the old-fashioned way." Sprout pulled out his lasso and flung the loop of rope at Mister Dark. The Mastercorp agent snatched the lasso out of the air and pulled, ripping the other end from Sprout's hands. Annoyed, Mister Dark chucked the lasso off the side of the dreadnought and charged at Sprout.

The boy drew his machete and aimed it at Mister Dark.

He didn't want to hurt the man, but he was running out of options. Mister Dark punched the machete, shattering it. Sprout dropped the hilt as the big man grabbed Sprout around the throat. "Now what are you going to do, little boy? What are you going to do?"

29

2-TOR ZIPPED THROUGH THE VENT. EVIE CLUNG TO HIM. IN THE DOCKING BAY BEYOND, LOADING arms crowded the pathways.

"Look out!" Evie cried. They crashed into the floor and slid across the room. Evie flopped onto her back, gasping for breath. The wind had blown her hair stiff, and she checked her arms and legs, amazed that nothing was broken.

"Toots?" asked a startled voice. "Is that you?"

Sitting up, 2-Tor turned his beak to the source of the voice. "Didi! My pink puffin. My fine feathered friend. My beloved booby!"

The pink robo-bird clacked her beak and flung her wings around 2-Tor. They hadn't seen each other since Evie and 2-Tor had been held captive on the dreadnought.

"Oh, Toots! You're here! You're alive! My personality matrix indicates that I am happy!"

"My CPU overheats for you, Didi!" 2-Tor cooed.

"2-Tor!" Evie clapped her hands together. "Mission!"

"Oh, most correct, Miss Evelyn." 2-Tor shook out his

feathers. "Didi, take us to the command center immediately. We must stop Mrs. Piffle and retrieve the Eden Compound."

"Toots . . ." Didi sighed. "She's not going to like that."

"Please," 2-Tor said. "It's the most important thing I'll ever ask of you."

"More important than asking me to marry you?" Didi huffed in offense. Evie giggled. The pink robo-bird really knew how to make the hard sell.

"I never said I would—" 2-Tor stopped short, then chuckled. "Oh, I see. Miss Didi, please take us to the command center. I promise I will make it worth your while."

With a twirl of her pink metal wings, Didi led the way out of the docking bay and through the corridors of the roboctopus. Evie felt a great sense of unease traveling these halls. Though the walls were solid metal, they seemed to thrum with the pulse of a beating heart. These pathways . . . were they Diana's veins?

They reached a doorway. Didi stopped. "Are you sure you want to do this? We could run away together, build a nest in a tree overlooking the sea, and not mess with Viola. I've gotta be honest with you, Toots, and you too, little girl, this lady is *mean*."

"Let us in, Didi," Evie insisted. She was ready. She knew she had to get to Vesuvia.

Didi opened the door. Inside the command center, big computer terminals lined the walls. Monitors projected camera feeds, news stations, and other information. Vats of bubbling Anti-Eden Compound stood in the four corners of the room.

At the front of the room, Vesuvia sat alone in a plain metal chair. She looked like a pale ghost of her former self, with a fearful expression on her face.

"Vesuvia!" Evie called, walking to her. "I found you! Listen, we need to talk. I know this is going to sound crazy, but you're the only one who can help us."

"I want . . . I can't . . ." The other girl shook her head in warning. "You have to get out of here. It's not safe!"

"You. I thought I had you killed."

At the sound of Viola's voice, Evie spun around but couldn't see her. Then, a flutter of wings caught her eye. Viola's mechanical ravens had concealed her in a dark corner of the room.

"Really, Vesuvia, do I have to do everything myself?"

Viola extended her arms and the ravens attacked. Their sharp metal wings slashed at Evie. One bladed feather nicked her cheek. She covered her face with her hands and pushed forward.

The birds surrounded Evie and pecked at her. The pain and weight pushed her to the ground.

"Miss Evelyn!" 2-Tor called out to her. He and Didi fought through the storm of ravens to reach the fallen girl, but Viola was ready. With a tap of her bracelet she fired an electromagnetic pulse at 2-Tor and Didi that was designed to disable machines. As the blue electricity coursed over their bodies, the two robots shook violently and crashed to the floor.

Evie leaped to her feet and dove at Viola. She fell short. The ravens snatched Evie by the back and plucked her from the ground. They carried her to Viola, who studied Evie as she dangled helplessly. Growling, Evie swung at Viola, trying to grab her.

"Oh, Evie, useless as ever," Viola shook her head. "But don't worry. I'll make you useful yet."

30

IT WAS NOT EASY CONTROLLING THE HOVERSHIP ALONE. WITH ONE HAND, RICK PILOTED THE VEHICLE. With the other, he aimed and fired the water cannon. Somehow, this worked.

"Look out, Ricky!" a warm and familiar voice warned him over the comm.

Rick swung his controls and the hovership spiraled out of the way of a missile. The bug that shot the missile swung around, but as it tried to line up a shot, a huge glob of soap suds flew through the air and smashed into the bug. Disabled, it fell to the earth far below.

He looked around for his rescuer and found his mother flying a single-seat hovership. "Come on, honey! I couldn't let you have all the fun! Let's clean up these dirty scoundrels together!"

Rick grinned, and together, mother and son took to the skies, shooting down bugs left and right. The rest of the fleet fought hard as well, and soon the bugs were on the run.

Rick wiped the sweat off his forehead. Now the hardest part was going to be waiting to see if Evie got the formula. They may have pushed back Mastercorp's fleet, but without the Eden Compound, there was no way for them to win.

THE WINTERPOLE HOVERSHIPS ZOOMED AROUND THE MASTERCORP DREADNOUGHT, BUT NEXT TO the massive vessel, they looked like gnats and were about as effective. Opening its great mouth, the dreadnought launched a volley of Anti-Eden Compound bombs. Ahead, the unsuspecting Los Angeles coastline was struck violently by the destructive projectiles. Silvery compound exploded across the landscape, reducing palm trees to iron filings and fleeing people to metal statues.

Seeing the destruction, Sprout couldn't take it any more. With a burst of strength, he broke free of Mister Dark's grip and ran across the deck. The large Mastercorp agent ran after Sprout, his metallically enhanced legs reaching him in just seconds. Mister Dark lunged, but Sprout spun out of the way so that he only caught a fistful of air.

"Hold still!" Mister Dark ordered.

"You gotta catch me," Sprout said with a wink.

They played this game for several minutes. Mister Dark

charged, Sprout rolled out of the way, avoiding capture, and Mister Dark roared in frustration.

Finally, panting heavily, Mister Dark pulled out another bottle of his serum and guzzled it. He threw the vial on the ground and it shattered. He howled in pain. As his breathing grew labored, his muscles began to expand and his silver thighs became so thick that they shredded his dress pants.

Mister Dark then stomped across the deck, each footstep shaking the platform and making Sprout lose his balance. The fierce wind whipped at them. Mister Dark's tattered clothes danced.

"I'm too quick for you, partner." Sprout backed away, trying to keep distance between him and the agent. His plan to distract Mister Dark was working, but if Mister Dark grabbed him it would be all over.

Even faster now, Mister Dark charged forward, barreling his shoulder into Sprout's chest. He groaned. It was like being hit by a hovership. The boy flew through the air and landed on his back, dangerously close to the edge of the dreadnought.

A spray of blue ice struck Mister Dark from above. One of the Winterpole hoverships bravely circled the deck.

"Freeze, you lout!" Barry shook his fist from the copilot seat of the hovership. "Mess with Winterpole and you'll get the avalanche."

"Nice, Barry!" Larry said approvingly. "That's a nice catchphrase you got there."

"Learned from the best, Larry." Barry patted his companion on the shoulder as they sped off, luring the bugs further away.

Mister Dark flexed, shattering the ice. He tore off his coat and shirt to remove the residue of the icetinguisher. Sprout scooted away from the edge.

"No more games." Mister Dark gasped for breath. He drank another bottle of the serum. The liquid splashed across his face. His skin tightened. With a roar, he leaped several dozen feet into the air. For a second, Sprout gaped in awe at this inhuman feat, then ran out of the way as the big man crashed into the deck. Mister Dark was so heavy that his feet broke through the metal exterior of the ship, trapping himself up to his waist. Mister Dark pounded the ground with his fists, struggling to escape.

At the rear of the ship, the sounds of several hundred icetinguisher blasts told Sprout the dreadnought's engines had been successfully disabled. Sprout breathed a sigh of relief. His plan had worked. He had distracted Mister Dark long enough to allow Winterpole time to attack the dreadnought.

Mister Dark struggled to punch through the metal hull to reach the vial in his pocket, but his hand was stiffening. In fact, his whole body was becoming rigid, turning completely into metal. "I just need a little more . . ." he groaned, then slumped over as the silver overtook his face, his metal body fusing with the broken hull of the dreadnought.

The Winterpole squadron flew overhead. Mister Snow's hovership lowered a ladder, and Sprout hopped on. He wasn't surprised that something as unnatural as what Mister Dark had been doing didn't work out.

As the hovership took off again, Sprout watched the dreadnought plummet to the surface of the ocean. It crashed with a great splash and then bobbed on the water. Sprout grinned victoriously. They'd have to do something about the wreckage. He wondered if it could be turned into a floating island off the coast of the eighth continent.

32

THE DISSONANT SCREECH OF HER MOTHER'S RAVENS FILLED VESUVIA'S HEAD WITH PAIN. THE red-eyed monsters surrounded the bubbling vat of Anti-Eden Compound, watching with anticipation as Viola hooked Evie Lane onto the chain and raised her into position. Arms at her sides, Evie struggled against her bonds, but couldn't escape. She swung like the trussed-up prey of a spider, waiting to be devoured. Just like Diana.

It was happening again. Vesuvia looked at the floor where the disabled robot bodies of 2-Tor and Didi were sprawled. Poor Didi. Vesuvia had never meant for her to suffer.

"Vesuvia! You idiot! Give me a status report on the battle outside," Viola screamed.

"Mastercorp's forces have been beaten back by the attacking hoverships," Vesuvia said hollowly as she looked at the viewscreen monitors. "We lost. They are retreating."

"What?" Viola asked. "Impossible! We are far more powerful than our enemies."

One of the monitors switched over from the battle to a news report. Vesuvia numbly noted that the news anchor had fabulous earrings and a sharp, stylish outfit, but she was too depressed to care. Facing the camera, the anchor said, "Thanks, Don, for that informative report. If you are just joining us, damage to the California coast is minimal, and the threat of continued attack has been neutralized. And now, SuperNews brings you an exclusive interview with the CEO of Mastercorp. In the effort of full disclosure, we would like to remind our viewers that SuperNews is owned in part by Infocommunicorp, a subsidiary of Mastercorp. Sir, welcome to the studio."

"It's great to be here, Cathy."

Vesuvia watched in surprise as the image on the monitor pulled back to reveal the CEO of Mastercorp. It was strange to see his head normal sized, but the man sitting across from the news anchor was unmistakably the same person that Vesuvia had seen giving orders to her mother.

The CEO spoke, looking concerned. "I want to make it absolutely clear, Cathy, Mastercorp had nothing to do with the tragic incidents happening today. Our internal investigation shows that a rogue executive, Viola Piffle, acted alone when she issued the order to attack Los Angeles and the eighth continent. As far as we know, Mrs. Piffle is a madwoman and we are doing everything we can to bring her to justice."

The news anchor nodded. "That is good news to hear, sir. We've just received word that the president issued a statement condemning the actions of Mrs. Piffle but commending you and the rest of Mastercorp's board of directors for speedily dealing with the bad apple in your bunch."

"That's what we do, Cathy," the CEO said. "We neutralize threats."

One of the ravens flew into the monitor, shattering the image of the CEO's face.

"Vesuvia, stop rotting your brain with *television*," Viola snarled. "Get up here and make yourself useful for once."

Vesuvia slowly joined her mother on the catwalk surrounding the vat of Anti-Eden Compound. She looked up at Evie, who dangled over the bubbling silver liquid.

"The CEO doesn't know what he's talking about. We are facing some setbacks," Viola explained. "But it's not over yet. I think all we need is an attack robot to destroy our enemies for good. But what kind of giant hideous robot animal should Miss Lane here be? A snarling warthog? A hyena? No, something even more annoying. Hmm . . ."

"Vesuvia," Evie begged. "Please, don't do this. You can stop it. You can help us. You can save Diana. You know where we can find the formula for the Eden Compound."

"Enough begging." Viola turned to Vesuvia. "I told you to kill Evie Lane, but you were weak and you failed. Now you get to enjoy the show."

She tapped the computer terminal. The chain began to lower Evie into the vat. "No! No! Help me!" Evie screamed.

Vesuvia tensed up, feeling the guilt of what happened to Diana weighing on her. It was like she was failing her all over again. She was so stupid. She should have done something.

"Help!" Evie screamed. She tried to lift her legs so she wouldn't touch the bubbling compound. The robotic arms came down and grabbed her, holding the girl in place.

Enough.

Vesuvia snatched her mother's bracelet, tearing it off her wrist.

"Stop that!" her mother hissed. "Give me that!"

The ravens squawked hysterically. Their tiny mechanical heads darted back and forth, looking between Vesuvia and her mother.

Vesuvia pushed the red button on the bracelet, and there was a rush of black metal wings. The ravens flew at Viola, pecking, swiping, biting her hair, perching on her from every angle.

"Stop! Let go! Get off me!"

Vesuvia pressed the button to call off the birds. But it wasn't responding. She pressed it again, then struck the bracelet with her palm, trying to make it work. Nothing.

"Ah! You monsters!" Viola flailed as the birds descended, covering her completely. They formed a tight shell around her, muffling her words. When the birds had all found a place to perch, the mass of mechanical ravens was still.

Vesuvia broke the silence. "Mom?" she asked.

The ravens took off. They flew straight through the front viewport, shattering the transparent barrier. They flew through the hole and vanished into the sky. Nothing remained of Viola Piffle.

Tears spilled freely from Vesuvia's eyes. She hadn't meant for that to happen. She only wanted her mother to stop, for all the madness to stop. Vesuvia wiped her eyes. She wasn't crying from sadness, but relief. It was over. She was finally free of her mother.

Vesuvia ran to the computer terminal and stopped Evie from descending into the vat. The robotic arms ceased their movement. Evie hung, staring down at Vesuvia.

"Hi . . ." she said.

"Hi," Vesuvia whispered.

She helped Evie down. Together, the two former enemies reactivated Didi and 2-Tor.

"I say! I seem to have fallen asleep!" 2-Tor said as he jolted awake.

"Oh, Toots!" Didi flung her wings around him. "Thank goodness your memory bank isn't fried."

"Vesuvia, we need the Eden Compound formula," Evie said.

"I know where it is," Vesuvia said. "I'll show you."

"Thank you," Evie's voice sounded tight. "And . . . just . . . thank you."

Vesuvia felt a strange feeling in her chest, a new feeling, like she was doing something *right*.

"Look at this!" Evie ran over to the wall of monitors. "Rick won! And Sprout too! We've defeated Mastercorp." She turned back to Vesuvia. "Will you come back with us? We need to get the formula to my dad so we can turn Diana back."

Vesuvia's eyes lit up. If they could save Diana, it would all be worth it.

33

A SMALL GROUP GATHERED AROUND THE HEAD OF THE GIANT PINK OCTOPUS FORMERLY KNOWN as Diana Maple. Rick, Evie, Sprout, Vesuvia, Mrs. Maple, and even 2-Tor and Didi wanted to be with Diana as Dad administered the newly re-created Eden Compound. As a precaution, the two robot lovebirds carried grass-woven umbrellas so they wouldn't accidentally get Eden Compound on them.

Rick was nervous. The potential for side effects was high. All sorts of robots and other machines had been placed or grown inside of Diana. They had cleaned all that stuff out—but what would the result be after she changed back? If she changed back. Rick shivered.

The *Condor* flew high above the enormous pink octopus. This was the moment of truth.

The Eden Compound spilled out the back of Dad's hovership, coating the octopus in the green substance. It rained down around them, striking the ground. Where the compound hit the remaining prefab buildings Mastercorp had placed, the structures turned to dirt and wood and stone, becoming quaint—if repetitive—little huts.

The group watched anxiously as Diana's tentacles began to retract and fuse together. The round pink head deflated, shrinking, revealing clearer facial features. "Diana . . ." Vesuvia sighed happily when she could recognize her friend's face again.

Moments passed. The octopus got smaller and smaller. The pink color faded. Vesuvia ran forward; Rick and the others followed. The transformation had been reversed. Diana Maple was a human girl again. Her eyes were closed.

Vesuvia leaned down and listened. "She's breathing!"

The others heaved a sigh of relief.

Diana stirred. She opened her eyes and looked around at everyone there. "Vesuvia? Rick? I . . . Why do I have a craving for shellfish?"

Rick laughed. He was so happy he felt like screaming from a mountain peak. "We'll explain everything soon. For now, we're glad you're safe."

Diana raised her eyebrows as Vesuvia pulled her into a tight hug. "Okay!" Diana said in surprise, patting her old friend's shoulder. "Wow, um . . . Nice to see you too."

"Yeah," Vesuvia said. "Ditto."

ONE YEAR LATER . . .

Scifun bustled with activity. From Evie's window in Spire One, she could see it all: the workers rushing about, the scientists' playful arguing, the students enjoying recess. The city existed in harmony with nature—the finest city on earth.

Evie zipped up her jumpsuit. She shouldered her bag. She nodded in satisfaction as she took one last look around her bedroom and left.

Down in the courtyard, Vesuvia was hunched over a worktable, surrounded by a team of architects, builders, and artists.

"Now this mile of the beach I have sectioned off, earmarked for double-decker ocean construction." Vesuvia circled a few key spots on the map in front of her. "We'll build wireless stations here and here, and smoothie bars here, here, and here."

"Working on a new project, Vesuvia?" Evie asked as she walked by.

"You bet!" Vesuvia said with a smile. "New New Miami is going to be the prettiest, coolest, bestest city on the whole continent."

Evie looked around at the fountains, topiaries, and other beauties of Scifun. "I dunno . . . I think you've got some competition."

Vesuvia laughed. "See you at the ceremony, Evie."

As Evie continued her walk, Diana fell into step with her, wearing her crisp white Winterpole senior agent uniform. "Good morning, Evie."

"Hi!" Evie replied. "What's up?"

"The Director would like to see you before the ceremony. Would you come with me to headquarters?"

Evie shrugged. "Of course!"

She followed Diana on a winding path through the city, arriving soon at a great glass structure that looked like an iceberg. It was the new headquarters of Winterpole.

Diana and Evie went inside. They didn't need permission. Diana led the way to the door to the Director's office. She poked her head in and then smiled at Evie. "The Director will see you now."

Inside the office, a high-backed executive office chair turned and Rick stood up from his seat.

"Hey, Mister Director," Evie grinned.

Rick adjusted his glasses. "Nice to see you too."

After the final battle with Mastercorp, the Director of Winterpole had decided it was time to retire at last. He could think of no one better to run the organization than Rick

Lane. Rick balanced his time between the Science Circle and Winterpole, although the truth was there was a good chance he wouldn't be on the Science Circle much longer. The rest of the family had already vacated their seats. The population of Scifun had grown into the millions, and although the citizens appreciated everything the Lane family had done, the eighth continent was bigger than them now. That's what happens in a democracy.

"Are you sure about this plan?" Rick asked.

"You had to try to talk me out of it one last time, huh?" Evie winked at him. "I'm sure, big bro."

Rick laughed, and they were quiet for a minute. Evie felt his eyes on her, watching and thinking.

Diana checked her watch and frowned.

"Sorry to interrupt, but it's time," she said.

The trio walked across the city to the Scifun Airport, where a crowd of thousands had gathered. When they saw Evie, they started screaming and cheering. She couldn't believe it. She had expected a small family gathering. What was this?

Rick and Diana made a path for Evie through the crowd, to the huge rocket at the center. Everyone wanted to high-five Evie or shake her hand.

Along the way, she spotted Doctor Mahmoun, from Doctor Grant's sun farm. He held Niels Bohr close. The cat's fur had grown back, and he gave Evie a soft meow.

Doctor Mahmoun said, "We came to see the big event. But this guy told me he wants to go with you."

Evie snorted. "Oh, he said that, did he?"

"Yes, miss," Doctor Mahmoun said, handing the cat to her. "He doesn't want you to get lonely."

"Well who am I to refuse this handsome guy?" Evie asked, cradling Niels Bohr in her arms. They continued on, together.

In the middle of the crowd, at the base of the rocket, Evie's parents stood with Sprout. Evie looked up at the tall stack of columns that made up her ship. At the top was her new home. At the bottom, Dad's latest experimental hover engine.

"The last round of tests went beautifully," Dad assured her, stepping forward to give her a hug. "You're gonna have a great time."

"I know I will, Dad. Thanks."

Sprout looked like he was about to cry. "I'm gonna miss you much too much, I reckon."

"I'm gonna miss you too, Sprout. But it won't be forever." After a long warm hug, he pulled off his cowboy hat and stuck it on her head.

"For luck," he said.

Evie didn't want to drag on her goodbyes. It would just make things harder. She placed Niels Bohr on her shoulder, then reached for the ladder that led up to the cockpit.

"Are you sure we can't change your mind?" her mother asked.

Evie turned. "I have to go. This whole adventure— it's been about the eighth continent, about exploring. We traveled the world, made a new one, brought joy to all these people. But now . . ." Evie looked out at the sea of people who had come to Scifun because of the dream and the promise of the eighth continent. Evie smiled at her mom. "Now I have to see what other worlds are out there to explore. Who knows? Maybe with this rocket's stash of Eden Compound, I can turn distant, barren planets into places as fertile as the eighth continent."

Evie began the long climb up the ladder. The crowd below chanted her name. Evie stopped and looked down at her family and friends.

"Hey, Rick," she said. "Take good care of our continent."

Rick nodded. He would.

Evie reached the top of the ladder and entered the rocket ship that would take her on a journey into the vastness of space over the next several years. She initiated the take-off sequence. Soon the whole ship rumbled violently and launched into the air. Evie fell back against her seat. The rocket passed through the atmosphere, leaving Scifun, the eighth continent, and the earth behind.

Evie set her trajectory, kicked in the afterburners, and flew into the starry light.

ACKNOWLEDGMENTS

I want to thank Ben Schrank and Gillian Levinson, as well as all the fantastic folks at Razorbill and Penguin Random House who helped to shape The 8th Continent. Ben gave me this chance and trusted all my crazy ideas. You would not be reading this without Gillian's creativity and smart critiques. Thank you also to the Penguins who worked so hard to make these books, especially Casey McIntyre, Vivian Kirklin, Krista Ahlberg, Lindsey Andrews, and Carmela Iaria.

A novel is only as good as its editors, which means my books were triply good. Thank you to Marissa Grossman for believing in my vision, and Tiffany Liao for her thoughtful comments and for sharing her love of The 8th Continent with me. You make my madness look good.

Thanks are owed to Sara Crowe and Harvey Klinger for their guidance and for connecting me with this project. Thank you to my agent Joanna Volpe for her friendship and wisdom, and to Jaida Temperly and the rest of the New Leaf team for always having my back.

Capstone Studios designed the sweet 8th Continent logo. The awesome artist Max Kostenko drew the cover art. His illustrations inspired these books a great deal. Courtney Wood created the 8th Continent website. The cool people at Funbrain made the game, shout outs to Michelle Teravainen and Caryn Blatt.

I want to thank my teachers and classmates from the Clarion Workshop, especially Grady Hendrix for his generosity and thoughtful conversations. Thanks to the New York Geek Posse past and present for their friendship and support. Let that be a lesson to all you aspiring scifi writers out there. The sooner you are proud to be a geek, the faster you'll find the coolest friends you'll ever know.

At its heart, The 8th Continent is a story about family and what a family can accomplish when they work together. I dedicated these books to mine, to my parents and brothers, my grandparents and aunts and uncles and cousins, and all my extended family. They taught me the importance of having a big brain, a bigger sense of humor, and the biggest heart. Sound like another family you know?

As always, the greatest thanks of all go to my partner in books and in life, Jordan Hamessley. You are my guardian and my voice. This one is for you.

They're all for you.

With love,
MATT LONDON
November 16th, 2015
New York, New York

MATT LONDON (themattlondon.com) is a writer, video game designer, and avid recycler who has published short fiction and articles about movies, TV, video games, and other nerdy stuff. Matt is a graduate of the Clarion Writers' Workshop, and studied computers, cameras, rockets, and robots at New York University. When not investigating lost civilizations, Matt explores the mysterious island where he lives—Manhattan.

Find out more at
8THCONTINENTBOOKS.COM